BONE QUILL

John and Carole E. Barrowman

First published in Great Britain in 2013 by
Buster Books, an imprint of
Michael O'Mara Books Limited
This Large Print edition published 2013
by AudioGO Ltd
by arrangement with
Michael O'Mara Books Limited

www.hollow-earth.co.uk

ISBN: 978 1471 338045

Printed and bound in Great Britain by
MPG Books Group Limited

'Then a powerful demon,
a prowler through the dark
nursed a hard grievance.'

Seamus Heaney, *Beowulf*.

*With love
to
Bud and Lois
and
Gavin*

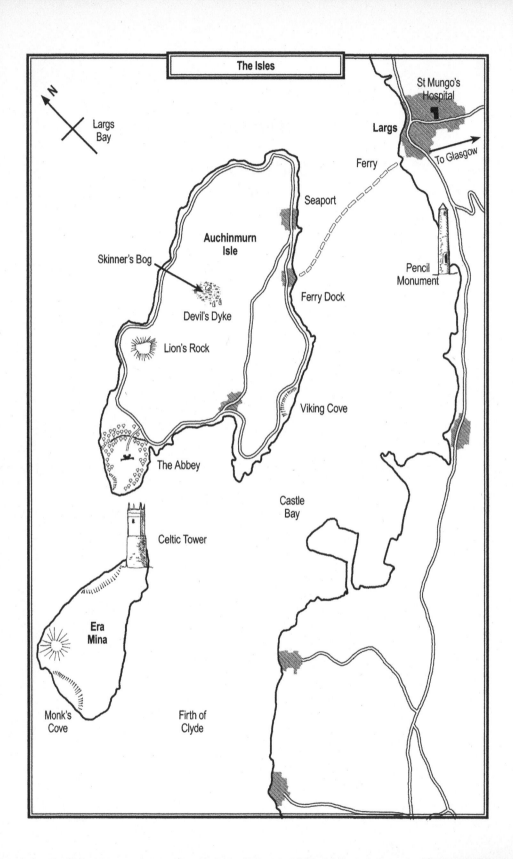

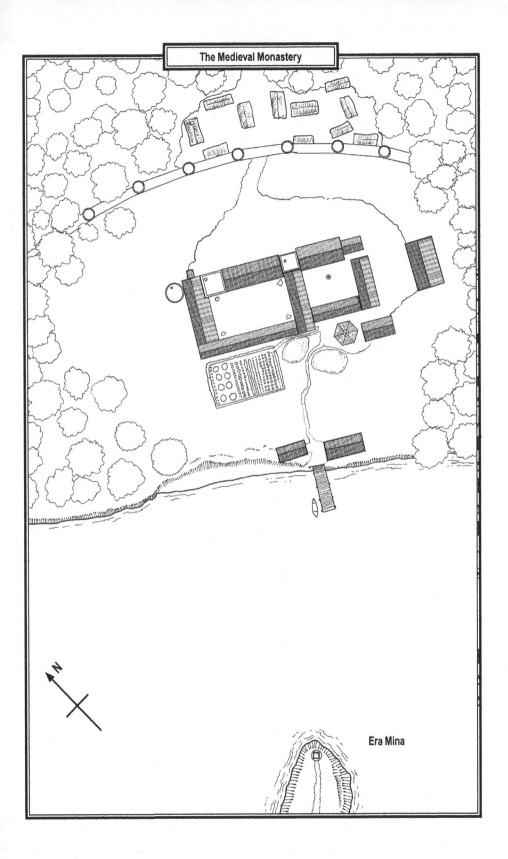

The Medieval Monastery

Era Mina

THE STORY SO FAR

Present Day

The events of the last couple of months for twins Matt and Emily Calder have been life-changing. Fleeing London with their mother for their grandfather Renard's protection on the Scottish isle of Auchinmurn, they learn that their mother Sandie is an Animare and their father Malcolm a Guardian, giving the twins an explosive combination of talents. Malcolm, increasingly obsessed by his ambition to free the beasts of Hollow Earth, was bound into a painting when the twins were young, but villains have already tried to use the twins' powers to free him. Thanks to the intervention of the white peryton—a magical creature tied to the history of Auchinmurn—the plot failed. But now the twins' mother has disappeared . . .

The Middle Ages

Fifteen-year-old novice monk Solon has helped the old Animare Brother Renard to free the magical white peryton from the sacred cave paintings on the small island of Era Mina. They strive to protect the monastery on Auchinmurn Isle and defeat Rurik the Red—a Viking leader in pursuit of a sacred relic he claims was stolen from his people. But the animation of the peryton has come at a cost, and

1

Brother Renard's imagination is fractured. And now, as the stonemasons are building a tower to keep Brother Renard safe, there are mutterings of rebellion among the other monks . . .

Turn to the Glossary on page 255 for further information.

PART ONE

ONE

The Abbey
Auchinmurn Isle
West Coast of Scotland
Ten Years Ago

The battle for control of the Calder twins' imaginations began on the afternoon of their third birthday. Sandie was enjoying the last slice of Jeannie's double-decker chocolate cake when Malcolm raced into the kitchen.

'I've found it!' he said, waving a red leather journal in front of Sandie in feverish excitement. 'Proof that Hollow Earth is real!'

Sandie's fork clattered to her plate. 'What?'

'It's all in this diary! *"The key must not be found"*—but this is the exciting part. Listen to this.' Malcolm flipped to another page. *"'After all that I have witnessed, after the horrors that have been revealed to me in Hollow Earth, I know this. The powers within are too terrible for man to control."*

'All these months of searching, and finally this!' He began to pace in front of the French doors. 'With Matt and Em's help, I—' He stopped, then turned and smiled at Sandie, '*We* will control Hollow Earth and then everything will be ours.'

'You're mad, Malcolm,' sputtered Sandie, dread creeping up her spine. 'I don't want everything.'

A part of Malcolm had always been wild—so

focused on his own obsessions that he ignored the feelings and opinions of others. Sandie had hoped marriage would calm him, but since the birth of the twins, this obsession with Hollow Earth had been eating away the Malcolm she'd fallen in love with.

'I don't care how you squander your powers or your life, but you can't use the twins to further this madness!' she went on, her pulse quickening. 'They're too young, practically babies. Their powers are not yours to control.'

Malcolm gripped Sandie's shoulders. She flinched. 'I won't be stopped by you or anyone else,' he said coldly. 'To master Hollow Earth is my destiny.'

* * *

The next morning, Sandie was glad of the chance to breakfast quietly with Renard, while Malcolm played with the twins outside. But as she gazed out of the window at the great glass sculpture in the Abbey grounds, she noticed something strange.

The sculpture was a massive mobile of mirrors suspended from the trees at the western point of the grounds, shimmering and spinning in the changeable winds that ran along the island's coastline. Matt and Em were sprawled under the installation on a blanket with their dad, painting. But what was reflected in the mirrors was not the cosy scene that it should have been. Instead, each shard was reflecting the swirling greens, browns and yellows of a mysterious cave mouth.

When the wind caught the mobile, the mirrored glass spun, and Sandie saw the tell-tale glow of an animation. A stabbing awareness pierced her mind.

She recognized the image.

Lasers of light suddenly shot from the cave mouth, every fragment of mirror multiplying the effects, creating a criss-crossing grid of light encasing the trees, trapping Malcolm and the twins inside.

'Renard!' Sandie screamed. 'Stop him!'

Renard Calder appeared at his daughter-in-law's side. He stared in shock at the scene unfolding on the lawn.

'My God, what's he doing?'

'I think he's using the mirrors to increase the twins' powers,' replied Sandie, her voice seared with panic. 'Malcolm has Duncan Fox's painting of the entrance to Hollow Earth, and the twins are animating it!'

'Impossible!' gasped Renard. 'That painting is locked in the vault.'

'When have locks—or even you—managed to stop your son?'

She raced through the French doors and across the wide lawn towards the trees that had lit up as if candles burned from their branches, with Renard close behind her.

'Stop!' Sandie screamed at the grid of light surrounding her children. She jabbed her finger into one of the light beams, yelping and drawing back when a shock shot up her arm and exploded in a million red dots in her head. Desperately searching for a way through the grid to reach the twins, she called out: 'Mattie, Emmie! Come over here to Mummy!' Once. Twice. Each time louder and more insistently.

The twins never budged, never looked up, never stopped painting. Malcolm was crouching next to them with his hands resting on their shoulders, his head close to their ears, whispering to them.

Renard pinched the bridge of his nose. 'He's inspiriting them. I can feel him.'

'How could he?' Sandie raced up and down, frantically scanning the neon cage, searching for a way inside. 'It's against everything we stand for. Everything!'

Matt and Em's tiny fingers were flying across their shared sketchpad. The gilt-framed painting of the cave mouth was propped next to them, beside another Fox painting of a scaly, hairless demon. Malcolm's knuckles were turning white, his fists clenched on the twins' slumped shoulders, holding them in place.

'What will his inspiriting do to them?' cried Sandie.

'I don't know.' Renard's face was white.

'Malcolm! Stop!' Sandie was crouching at the tree line, trying to catch Matt's or Em's attention, to break Malcolm's spell. 'Please! They're too young. You'll hurt them!'

The twins painted on, oblivious to the danger looming over them.

Malcolm slowly lifted his head. With eyes blazing, he looked over at Sandie, his handsome face contorted, his skin pale. Lifting his hand from Em's shoulder, he held a finger to his lips.

For Sandie the next seconds unfolded in horrifying slow motion. Matt and Em put down their paintbrushes and took each other's hands. They clambered to their feet, watching excitedly as the painting they'd been copying projected itself around them like a 3D movie, wrapping them in thick, swirling brush strokes of green, brown and yellow. At first the twins giggled at the lines of colour. But then the painting began to close in on them. Clinging to each other, their expressions quickly transformed from delight to apprehension.

'Daddy! I don't want to do this,' wailed Em.

'Make it stop,' cried Matt.

Fading into the churning colours, the twins disappeared completely. Sandie screamed and charged towards the grid. On the shards of mirrors shifting in the wind, Matt and Em's reflections appeared at the mouth of the animated cave.

'Go in! The key will be inside the cave. Bring it to me!' Malcolm shouted, shooing them inside with his hands.

'No!' Sandie shrieked.

She watched helplessly as the twins, tightly holding hands, vanished inside the cave. Malcolm's eyes blazed in triumph. Sandie collapsed on the grass. Renard was frozen to the spot.

After five agonizing minutes, the twins scrambled empty-handed from the cave. They were both crying.

With a roar of frustration, Malcolm tore up the painting. The air seemed to open above the blanket and the twins tumbled on to the grass among the fading lines of light.

Frantically gathering them up, Sandie wrapped her children in the blanket, cooing softly to them. Blood trickled from Matt's nose. Em's eyes were red-rimmed and unfocused. Neither of them spoke. They seemed to be in a trance.

'They'll be fine in the morning,' said Malcolm, mussing Matt's hair. 'Disappointing, though. I was sure that painting was where he'd hidden the key. Maybe it's in the other one.'

Renard pulled Sandie and the twins into his arms to comfort them. Malcolm began to laugh.

'You will eventually see things my way, Sandie,' he said. 'Our children will be capable of extraordinary things when they fully come into their powers. We will find Hollow Earth together!'

Renard stared at the expression on his son's face, and then at the still-blank faces of his grandchildren. 'You will never inspirit or harm these children again as long as I live, Malcolm,' he said.

'You're an old man, Dad,' grinned Malcolm. 'I may not have long to wait.'

Renard dropped his hands to his side, sending a wave of energy towards his son and knocking Malcolm off his feet. Malcolm crashed to the ground, cutting his head, and let out a feral howl as Renard sliced into his thoughts. The older man's eyes opened wide in anguish—and Malcolm pounced.

Renard pivoted in time to catch his son's arm, twisting him into a headlock and bringing him to his knees. Snarling, Malcolm sank his teeth into Renard's forearm, tearing at his flesh. The pain broke Renard's concentration, allowing Malcolm to pull away from his father's grip.

'These are my children,' screamed Malcolm. He wiped at the blood flowing from the cut on his head. 'I will decide their fate. Not you and not her!'

'No you will not!' said Renard, slamming into Malcolm's chest, knocking him against a tree. Malcolm's eyes slid shut at the impact.

The twins in their exhaustion were asleep, huddled in their mother's arms. Renard lunged for the sketchbook. Holding his bloody arm over a blank page, he let his blood pool on to it.

'What are you doing?' cried Sandie.

'We must bind him. Right now,' said Renard, pushing the unconscious Malcolm's hair from his forehead and letting the blood from the gash mingle on the page with his own.

Sandie laid the sleeping twins down and knelt in front of Renard, her hand on his. 'We can't . . . the consequences if we're discovered . . . They don't bear thinking about.'

Renard lifted his eyes to Sandie's. His shame and sadness for what he was about to do robbed Sandie of her breath.

'We must . . . we must . . .' Renard struggled for words. 'When I tried to get into Malcolm's head to calm him, I saw the most awful things. Demonic beings clawing up from the bowels of the earth, an army of rotting corpses lurching behind them. I saw beasts battling above the sea, their massive wings churning tidal waves beneath them . . .' He paused, handing the page to Sandie. 'And I saw Matt and Em awash in their own blood. My son is a monster. He must be stopped. Do it before he wakes up!'

Malcolm groaned, his eyes fluttered. Sandie stared at the other Fox painting Malcolm had left on the blanket. The monster Malcolm had become deserved to be bound in a painting of a horrible scaly demon. Seizing one of the twin's paintbrushes, she cleaned it with shaking fingers, dipped it into the blood on the page and began to copy the skinless monster.

Renard put his hand on her shoulder and closed his eyes. The wind picked up, the air smelled of seaweed and a hint of pine tar. The paintbrush felt hot. Sandie's skin began to blister as she outlined

11

the demon in Malcolm's and Renard's blood. Keeping the brush at the heart of the canvas, Sandie let Renard's power surge through her animation.

The trees rustled. The waves slapped the shore. A ghostly silhouette coiled up from the page. It hovered above Malcolm's head, tendrils snaking over him, embracing him, coating him in darkness. Malcolm slowly began to fade, his being absorbed into the animation, binding him in its form.

TWO

The Monastery of Era Mina
Auchinmurn Isle
Middle Ages

Solon sprinted down the corkscrew steps from the Abbot's tower and out into the monastery's courtyard. He hesitated for a moment. This place of sanctuary had been a place of death and destruction only days earlier. The cobbles that had run red with blood had been sluiced clean, but the smell of death still lingered like carrion. The occasional moans of the injured drifted from Brother Cornelius's infirmary.

Staying beneath the wall-walk, Solon crossed quickly to the entrance to the chapel and slid inside. He scanned the three empty rows of benches facing the unadorned half-moon altar and exhaled slowly, allowing himself a moment of respite from his nagging fears. He didn't know why he was feeling so afraid, so out of sorts—but he was. Despite having vanquished Rurik the Red and his Viking brutes, Solon sensed some of the monks were watching him; that the Vikings had disturbed a balance among the Order. Most troubling of all, deep in his mind Solon believed that the island had been wounded that day, and somehow he was expected to heal it.

On the altar stood three wooden coffins, holding

the remains of the monks murdered during the Viking attack. Their bodies had been embalmed and wrapped in strips of sackcloth, the wrappings sealed with beeswax. Only their faces were visible, waxy and pale, their closed eyes already sunken like dark craters. An apron of candles burned at their feet. They would soon join their predecessors down in the monastery catacombs.

As he was about to push through the heavy oak door behind the altar and head inside the monastery, Solon heard raised voices. He ducked behind the altar.

Tam and Rab came through the door, rags tied around their faces to mask the sickly sweet stench of embalming fluid. Solon recognized the village embalmers and was about to reveal himself when Tam spoke.

'If ye ask me, we shouldn't be worrying about the dead so much, Rab. Not after what I've heard.'

Rab's shaved head and pocked skin made him look like a troll. 'What have you heard?'

Tam dropped his voice to a whisper. 'I think the Vikings left a spy. Some of the monks saw a stranger wandering the hillside not long after the attack.' He glanced over his shoulder at the bodies before yanking Rab off to the side as if the dead were eavesdropping. 'And that's not all. The relic the Vikings were looking for? They were forced away without it. They'll be back worse than before once the stranger has spied out our weaknesses. Mark my words.'

A gust of wind blew open the door. Solon saw the two men jump with fright.

'If a spy is in our midst,' said Rab, recovering first and hiking his trousers up over his soft paunch,

14

'it would explain the strange goings on since the attack. Food's been getting pinched, and more than the usual—'

'Aye,' interrupted Tam, 'and my lad who empties the slop pails has seen more than one monk recently forgetting where he was and what he's supposed to be doing, as if he were under some kind of spell. I'm thinking the Viking gods cursed our island.' He pulled a pouch stuffed with smashed roots and herbs from under his shirt. 'This'll ward away the devil himself.'

'Aye,' said Rab, quickly touching the edge of the pouch before Tam settled it back under his tunic. 'But aren't we better prepared than we were? We've erected beacons along the coastline, and the Abbot has put his best archers on the wall.'

Tam scanned the chapel. 'Fat lot of good all that'll do us if a spy betrays our defences.'

Solon shifted his position, making his boots squeak on the stone flags behind the altar. Instantly, Rab lifted his hammer from his belt, and Tam slipped his knife from its sheath. They inched slowly towards where Solon was hiding. Tam was about to lean over the wooden altar table when one of the kitchen cats darted out from under a front pew.

Both men laughed and relaxed. Then they attended to the job at hand, nailing the lids on to the coffins and carrying the dead to the crypt.

Solon stopped holding his breath when the door swung shut behind them. Until the attack, he had found the monastery of Era Mina to be a place of solace and protection. Now it was becoming a bubbling cauldron of secrets and suspicions. A cauldron that was about to boil over.

THREE

The Abbey
Auchinmurn Isle
Present Day

On the massive corkboard near the sitting-room door, there was a photograph of Matt, Em and their mother taken in front of a fountain in London a year ago, before their lives had changed. They all looked so happy, ignorant of what was about to happen. Matt stared at the photograph for a long time, trying hard to separate his longing for his missing mum from his anger at what she had done to his dad.

He felt his sister's thoughts in his head.

Mum's okay, Matt. Wherever she is, I feel that she's okay.

You don't really know that, Em.

You're right. But I trust that Mum left us for a reason. When we figure out exactly what that was, then we'll find her. I know we will.

'I'd like to be anywhere but here, in this room, in this Abbey,' said Matt aloud.

Em was finishing a panel of sketches at the drafting table that sat in front of the sitting room's tall windows. She was creating a comic book about their recent adventures. 'How about bikes?' she offered, her eyes on her work. 'We could make a motocross track in the woods again. You and Zach are getting pretty good.'

'Maybe,' answered Matt, 'but the track's beyond the wall.'

He glanced irritably at the swirling ribbons of white fog seeping like dry ice in and around the high medieval wall that enclosed the Abbey compound. The fog was an animated force-field powerful enough to trap any intruding animation and reduce it to its base elements of light and colour.

During the day, the shield continually animated itself into any number of logical and obvious things that might be found on the high stone wall of an historic Celtic abbey. Yesterday, the postman had seen thick vines of ivy, and commented to Jeannie, the Abbey's housekeeper, on the beautiful white flowers that had somehow managed to blossom between the stones despite the thickness of the wall. The day before, a school group visiting the island had bicycled past, cheering in appreciation at the festive flags and colourful streamers threaded between the stones.

At night, the white mist oozing from the walls took on an eerie bluish tint. Anyone looking closely assumed that the vapour was the phosphorescent glow generated by spotlights anchored next to the hellhound gargoyles on the wall's perimeter.

Of course, the smoky animation was also designed to interfere with any animations the twins might try to create in order to get outside the Abbey grounds themselves. They were not so much in prison as protective custody, but the distinction made little difference to Matt. Either way, he was trapped; and when he felt trapped, he felt powerless; and when he felt powerless,

17

he felt hostile.

'I can't stand being cooped up any longer,' he said, flipping through a stack of video games sitting next to the flat-screen TV. He discarded them one at a time without any concentrated consideration of the titles.

'Oh, would you please stop fidgeting!' said Em. She was applying a tint to a panel of a beautiful flying stag—a peryton. 'You know we can't go anywhere.'

Even on the paper, Em's peryton pulsed with energy. She had shaded its body in a pure white and was smudging a light grey charcoal crayon across the surface to 'pop' its massive wings.

Matt turned the pad so he could examine the image. 'Aren't you afraid you'll animate that? Simon would not be happy if he had to repair another set of stained-glass windows.'

When the peryton had last appeared on Auchinmurn, it had crashed through a massive stained-glass window in one of the converted cloisters of the medieval monastery that had once stood on the site of the Abbey.

An expression of annoyance crossed Em's face. 'You may not have been paying attention in our lessons recently, but I have. If we want to continue to develop as artists, we have to learn to control our Animare abilities when we draw, so that every drawing we create doesn't come alive. The First Rule, remember? Never animate in public.'

She turned the pad back round. 'I'm practising so that I can draw without unintentionally bringing something to life. You should be practising, too.'

'I don't need to,' snapped Matt.

Em wasn't about to admit this aloud, but her

brother's assessment of his abilities was true. Matt's Animare powers were developing more quickly than hers, and although her Guardian abilities were stronger than Matt's, Em was not fully in control of her imagination all of the time. Matt, on the other hand, was much more able to disconnect, to turn his powers on and off.

You'll equal his abilities someday, Em. I know you will.

Em smiled at Zach. It was comforting to have him in her head—most of the time—and to know he was aware of how she felt, especially when sadness gripped her and she fretted for hours about her mum.

FOUR

A large picture on the opposite wall of the sitting room caught Matt's eye. 'Let's go back to London,' he said, waving at the painting. 'Just for a few minutes. I miss it. Don't you?'

Lip-reading from the couch, Zach jumped up. 'Oh, no! You're not going anywhere, and you're certainly not going into a painting.'

'Zach's right,' said Em nervously. 'We promised. No animating without supervision.'

'Forget that,' said Matt, standing the painting on the empty easel in the corner. He flipped to a clean sheet of paper on his sketchpad. 'No one will ever know.'

'I will,' signed Zach, stepping in front of the easel.

'You'd tell on us?' Matt challenged.

Em prepared to separate the boys if this escalated into a fight. 'I'm not helping you go into the picture, Matt,' she warned.

'I may not need you to.'

'You may be getting stronger, but you're not Leonardo da Vinci yet.'

'You can't stop me if I want to do it.'

'If you're so smart,' said Em, her annoyance building, 'then you should be able to tell I don't want to do this.'

'That's not true,' said Matt. He grinned at his sister. 'I know you'd like to go back to London,

20

even if it's only for a few minutes.'

His green eyes were filled with more excitement than Em had seen in weeks.

You're not seriously considering doing this, Em.

No, Zach . . . okay, maybe . . . I can't let him do it alone. That's not . . . that's not me. That's not us. We help each other. We always have, and especially now with Mum gone.

'Stop talking about me in your heads,' begged Matt, pulling his fingers through his long, dark hair in agitation. 'I can tell when you do that. I'm not completely clueless about you two.'

Em stared at the picture that Matt had placed on the easel. It was a study for Claude Monet's *The Thames below Westminster*: a beautiful, richly textured painting of the River Thames. The National Gallery in London had the final painting.

She had to admit, she did miss London.

'Em. No,' signed Zach in warning. He was aware that he couldn't stop the twins on his own if they decided to act together. Their combined powers as Animare were far too strong for his fledgling Guardian abilities. If they got into trouble, he doubted he could help them.

Picking up a crayon, Matt began to copy the painting, his nimble fingers whipping across the paper. First, he sketched the outline of Westminster and the impressive gabled arches of St Stephen's Tower, then the distinctive spire of Big Ben in the painting's soft but luminous background.

Keeping the image firmly in his imagination, Matt passed the impressive outline to Em, who glanced at Zach regretfully before grabbing a couple of pastels from the table and filling in the drawing.

21

'Well,' said Matt, looking at the wooden pier standing on stilts over the Thames. 'Are you going to tell on us or not, Zach?'

Zach gave a sigh of resignation. 'Not. But only if I can come into the painting with you.'

FIVE

The Monastery of Era Mina
Middle Ages

Solon sat in Brother Renard's isolated chamber, watching the old monk as he slept in his birch-branch rocking chair beside the roaring hearth. Brother Renard's skin had turned the colour of a ripe turnip, his hair had begun to fall out in clumps, and bursts of agitated zeal were followed by periods of exhaustion. All these changes saddened Solon more than he could say. Since the Abbot had made the agonizing decision to lock away Brother Renard and his fracturing imagination, the local stonemason had started work on a tower for the old monk on the northern tip of Era Mina, where he would be safe from the world and the world safe from him. Until its completion, Brother Renard was isolated here in the furthest corner of the darkest wing of the monastery, under Solon's watchful eye.

The only window in the room was barred with wooden shutters, the sunlight slipping in through the narrow slats. From the fire, a log spat and snapped like an angry hound. Two tall, carved candelabra lit the tiny room, their wax dripping on to the mantel in honey-scented drops. The air in the room was pleasant, if a bit stifling, the smells of the wax blending with the scent of heather from inside the bedrolls. For centuries, the women of the village had been stuffing bedding with heather and grass, believing the perfume warded off nightmares. It would take more than heather to ward off poor Brother Renard's. When an Animare lost control of his imagination, the loss caused far more damage inside the mind than out.

A knock at the door startled Solon to his feet. Visitors to the room were few. He lifted a brass key tied to a strip of leather under his tunic and unlocked the door to admit the visitor.

'Brother Cornelius!'

Solon liked the monastery's herbalist and healer, a short, stout monk with rosy cheeks, a wide, hooked nose and a clerical crown of tonsured red hair. Waddling into the room in his black robes, Brother Cornelius looked like the birds that nested on the island's cliffs. He had taught Solon which plants produced the brightest inks, which trees oozed the best resins, and which seeds could be ground for inks but never eaten.

Cornelius noted the dishevelled state of Brother Renard. 'I have a dangerous request, Solon,' he said. 'It's perilous, but a task the Abbot and I know you are more than capable of fulfilling.'

Solon sensed an odd stillness from Cornelius. The herbalist was exhausted, Solon decided, returning to his three-legged stool. It had been only three days since the Vikings had attacked the monastery, and Cornelius had been hard at work tending to the sick and injured.

The herbalist sat on the wider of the two bedrolls spread on wooden bunks, beside an embroidered quilt folded neatly at the foot of the bed.

'Has Brother Renard said much since the

attack?' asked Cornelius.

'He speaks a little. He asks about the wounded. He prays for the dead. I'm able to distract him with reading, but his mind rests more peacefully, of course, when his Guardian, the Abbot, is here.'

'Of course,' nodded Cornelius.

'How may I help you, Brother?' asked Solon.

The monk sighed. 'As you may have heard, many of the wounded from the Viking raid are not healing as quickly or as well as I had hoped. Many who are suffering are children, much younger than you. In the past, Brother Renard was wary of sending you to Skinner's Bog to gather plants, but I must ask you to go.'

Solon frowned. 'Why has Brother Renard not wanted me to go to Skinner's Bog?'

'Because the bog is the lair of the Grendel.'

SIX

Whether the ancient stories called it the mud-monster, the spirit-stalker or the Grendel, every peasant on Auchinmurn knew of the beast of Skinner's Bog. Solon had heard accounts of the Grendel since he was old enough to sit at the fire and listen to his elders. He doubted that such a creature could ever be as grisly and as foul a force as the storytellers claimed.

But before Solon could ask Cornelius anything more, Brother Renard woke. He slowly lifted his head and acknowledged his visitor with a nod. A clump of hair floated to the plank floor like a fuzzy insect.

'Cornelius, dear friend.'

Cornelius smiled fondly. 'I've come with a task for Solon.'

'Ah, the boy is certainly capable.'

'My apologies, master,' interrupted Solon, 'but why is it critical that I go to Skinner's Bog, Brother Cornelius?'

'Skinner's Bog?' said Brother Renard, suddenly glaring at Cornelius.

Solon felt the old monk's anxiety thumping behind his eyes.

'Because,' said Cornelius, 'it's the only place on the island with a rowan tree. I have no choice. I must have its berries to heal the wounded from the Viking attack before infection sets in.'

26

Brother Renard's eyes narrowed on Cornelius, his rocking increasing in speed. 'Not possible alone,' he muttered. 'Not possible with someone. Not possible at all.'

'The boy has proven himself to be valiant,' pointed out Cornelius.

'The boy has much still to learn,' said Renard, his agitation mounting.

'But because of your animation—because you used Solon, Brother—he is now the one connected to the peryton,' said Brother Cornelius. 'And you know as well as I do that the peryton can help him find the rowan tree.'

Solon was stoking the fire, listening carefully to the two monks as they argued.

'Some day very soon,' the Abbot had told him, 'when your master is able and ready, he will tell you the story of the islands and of our Order. It may well be his final lesson to you, but until then, know that you and your descendants are forever bound to the peryton and to the island of Era Mina.'

Solon had done his best to encourage, even cajole his master into teaching him this lesson, but his master had always ducked into his own dreams and silences, just when Solon thought he'd caught him at the right moment.

'The boy would be in mortal danger, even with the peryton,' snapped Renard at Cornelius.

The old monk's rocking was becoming more frenzied, and he was scratching his fingers across his lap as if writing on an invisible page. Leaping from his stool, Solon pressed his hands on Brother Renard's chair, trying to stop its frantic rocking, afraid of the old monk's rage and what might happen if he lost control.

27

'But Renard, he must go,' continued Cornelius pleadingly. 'Too many will suffer and die if he does not.'

'I won't allow it!'

'Renard, dear, dear friend,' said Cornelius. He leaned forward on the edge of the bunk, causing the quilt to slither to the floor. 'This is not your decision to make. It is Solon's.'

Suddenly, Brother Renard's chin dropped to his chest, and the chair settled. For a fleeting moment, Cornelius thought he had passed away, gone for ever. Then the old monk's hands started to move at lightning speed across his lap again.

'Look out!' yelled Solon.

A royal jester in full court regalia was rising out of one of the quilt squares, flopping his arms and twisting his legs as if they were made of soft clay. But where the jester's head should have been, there was nothing, only his tri-pointed cap resting on empty shoulders, a wide, gap-toothed grin leering from its centre.

'May the saints preserve us,' said Brother Cornelius.

Before the stout monk could get off the bunk, the headless jester sprang up into the air, stretched his arms to a ceiling beam, somersaulted over it, grinned malevolently and dropped on to Cornelius's shoulders, pinning him to the bed.

All in three blinks of Brother Cornelius's eyes.

Brother Renard's eyes, on the other hand, were squeezed closed in a kind of trance, the chair rocking furiously under him as he fought to contain his imaginings, his fists clenching and unclenching.

On the bunk, Cornelius was flailing madly to fight off the animation. The jester wrapped his loose legs around Brother Cornelius's waist and sprang from the bunk again, taking the terrified monk up to the ceiling beam. Cornelius's scream became a whimper when the jester dropped back down to the bed, leaving the herbalist clinging to the oak crossbeam, high above the floor.

SEVEN

'Let me try to . . . to animate a way down for you, Brother Cornelius,' called Solon, hunting frantically around the tiny room for something he could use to sketch.

He could find nothing. Then he remembered. The Abbot had stripped the room bare to avoid Brother Renard using any tools to animate.

Brother Renard was still rocking and shuddering. A thick, green beanstalk embroidered on the border of the quilt shot upwards, winding and knotting itself over and under the bunk, quickly smothering the headless jester in vines. The jester shook his jingling hat and exploded in a cloud of red and yellow stripes. The moment he had disappeared, the beanstalk grew directly up to the crossbeam and curled around it, sprouting thick, green leaves and white flowers above where Brother Cornelius was dangling.

'I believe in his own way,' shouted Solon to the terrified monk, 'that Brother Renard may be offering his assistance. He must be in a battle inside his own imagination.'

'I do appreciate Brother Renard's motives, but I've no intention of climbing down from this height on one of his shaky imaginings,' squeaked Brother Cornelius from the crossbeam. 'If it's all the same to you, Solon, I'll wait for a ladder.'

'It may be safer to come down when you can,'

called Solon. 'Who knows what may be next?'

There was a furious buzzing from the quilt. It was coming from a hive of honeybees swarming on one of the middle squares, their black and yellow bodies bulging furiously from the cloth.

'Oh my. They look angry,' said Brother Cornelius weakly.

With a piercing squawk, a fat puffin suddenly flew out of the beanstalk's foliage, swooped over Cornelius's head and defecated a blob of purple ink on his balding pate.

'Ach, for the love of God, Renard,' Cornelius cried, mopping his brow. 'Alright. Alright. I'm coming down.'

The Abbot suddenly burst through the door.

'Oh, Brother Renard!' he cried, pressing his fingers to his temples. 'What on earth has you so agitated?'

He took in the monastery's herbalist carefully climbing down a beanstalk, Solon standing underneath waiting to assist him, Renard rocking and scribbling, and a puffin that looked remarkably like Brother Cornelius leaving coloured droppings on every surface in the room.

The Abbot went to the window, threw open the shutters and shooed the puffin out into the evening sky where, at a short distance from the window, the bird broke up into a rainbow of feathers. Then he crouched down in front of the old Animare and took his hand, calming his imagination, controlling his thoughts, inspiriting him as only a Guardian can.

Immediately, the beanstalk dissolved in flashes of green, and Brother Cornelius fell heavily on top of Solon. The puffin's droppings disintegrated in clouds of purple paint, dusting Brother Cornelius, Brother Renard, the Abbot and Solon in a layer of stinky sprinkles.

EIGHT

London
1871

The twins tumbled on to a wooden pier that stretched like a gnarled finger over the River Thames. Light from the late afternoon sun filtered through the London smog and on to the choppy water, exactly as Monet had painted the scene and precisely how the twins had imagined it.

'Where's Zach?' asked Em, picking herself up off the timber jetty. They were alone on the pier, two tiny figures silhouetted against the muted majesty of a ghostly Westminster.

'Em, look!'

'Can you see him?' *Zach, where are you?*

'Not yet, but that's not what I mean. Check out the river!'

Em walked to the palings of the pier and looked downstream. 'Wow. That's some floating traffic jam.' She glanced back at Matt as realization dawned. 'Wait. That's not how it is in the painting. Monet painted only two or three small steamers on the river. There must be at least fifty boats out there.'

A line of barges piled high with coal navigated the middle of the Thames towards the factory docks to the east, their tall chimneys belching black smoke into the leaden sky. Smaller vessels were dodging in and out of the wake of the barges. Opposite the twins on the other side of the river was a line of rickety wooden cranes, standing in the middle of partially demolished red-brick warehouses.

'If we were in Monet's painting,' said Matt excitedly, 'then this scene would be as he painted it. But we can see outside the frame of his picture.'

'What are you—' Em began. She suddenly covered her mouth and nose with her hand. 'Oh my God, what is that disgusting stench?'

The air was rank with the stink of rotting fish, horse manure, unwashed bodies and coal tar. On the Victoria Embankment behind them, raw sewage was flowing in thin trenches and spewing into the river in lumps.

'I'm going to throw up.' She leaned over the palings, gagging.

Matt squeezed his sister's shoulders. 'Do you realize how amazing this is?' He sounded stunned. 'We're not in Monet's painting. I think we've travelled back in time to *when he painted it*. I bet if we followed the river downstream, we might actually find Claude Monet with his easel. We might even be the thin figures on the pier that he is painting right at this very moment.'

'Are you kidding me?' Em croaked. 'But . . . but how—'

A horse-drawn omnibus clanged its warning bell loudly as it trundled past the pier, red spiral stairs twisting to an open top deck filled to capacity with passengers, all of them breathing in the visible London smog. The surface of the road in front of the pier was mostly trampled soil, and was as bustling as the river.

'How can we do any of the things we've discovered we can do as Animare?' said Matt, wild with excitement. 'Grandpa said no one really knows how the combination of Mum's and Dad's Animare and Guardian abilities would affect us. All he said was that it would make our imaginations more powerful and more unique than anyone before us.'

Matt's eyes blazed at the scene around him, his black mood of earlier all packed up and stored beneath his rising excitement and pulsing adrenalin. 'Monet must have been an Animare. It's the only way this makes sense!'

Fear charged through Em's veins, muting the excitement Matt was projecting through her.

'Great,' she said. 'Now we're in seriously big trouble.'

NINE

Scanning the chaotic city scene for Zach, Em took in the big and small differences between this London and the one that she and Matt knew from their childhoods.

In this London, the pedestrians hustling along the Embankment were more formally dressed. Many of the men were in colourful waistcoats, knee-length frock coats and top hats; the women in full skirts layered over frilly petticoats, their heads topped with elaborate hats.

But in the middle of the wide street, vendors were in rags. Em noticed children of all ages everywhere, darting in and out of buildings, weaving along the middle of the busy road, sleeping in twos and threes under carts. And then there were the smells, like boiling cabbage and rotting flesh.

Concentrate, Em, she admonished herself. *Find Zach.* Her anxiety about what might have happened to him was mounting.

Zach! Can you hear me?

'You had a tight grip on him when we animated, didn't you?' she asked Matt.

'Of course!' Matt was too wired to focus on Em's fears. 'We linked arms as soon as the light burst in our heads. I felt him shifting with us. I know he's here.'

Zach!

36

'Everything is pulled by horses,' exclaimed Matt.

Em shook her head at his inability to focus when she really needed him to.

'I'm just *saying*. We have really time-travelled. How awesome is that? Like Doctor Who or Terminators.'

Suddenly, the wooden planks of the jetty began to tremble under their feet, and an explosive release of air like a powerful fire-hose erupted nearby.

'Oh, man,' said Matt, darting to the other side of the pier. 'Check that beast out.'

Charging across the Charing Cross Railway Bridge about a hundred metres downstream was a colossal steam train, its muscular engine coughing clouds of black smoke into the already severely polluted air.

'That's a really big train,' said Em.

'Duh!'

Em wiped a layer of soot from her sleeve where she'd leaned against the palings. 'If this really is nineteenth-century dirt, Matt, then our abilities are turning pretty scary.'

'*Scary*? Are you kidding me? More like amazing,' said Matt, jogging quickly down the shaky plank stairs and on to the Embankment. 'The London Eye should be on the other side of the river. That factory way down there becomes the Tate, and the Millennium Bridge should be there. None of these people has ever heard of traffic lights or telephones or computers or *Star Wars* or . . . this is so cool!'

Em yanked Matt under the jetty stairs as two fussily-dressed gentlemen passed them, staring at great length and with quite obvious contempt at the twins' attire. Matt was in a well-worn pair of baggy jeans and a vintage T-Rex rock T-shirt from his dad's wardrobe. Em was in cuffed skinny jeans, sparkling pink flats and three layered tank-tops. She'd never been so self-conscious in her life about her punk hair and her funky clothes.

'This city ought to treat the urchin population the way it treats the rats,' they heard one of the gentlemen sniff. 'Drown them all.'

'Hey!' Matt began indignantly.

Em held him back. 'Zach! Remember? We have to find him!'

The centre of the wide street directly in front of them was dotted with horse troughs and vendors with carts full of sad-looking vegetables, trays of herring, tatty leather boots, wool caps and a cart filled with books, papers and postcards. Shiny black and silver open carriages lumbered along the dusty road, hansom cabs darting between them. Men in grey suits and bowler hats and one or two women in sweeping skirts and boleros rushed like ants in and out of the buildings of Whitehall: official Parliament buildings the same then as now.

Or should it be the same now as then? Em thought.

Angry at her own distractions, she scanned the busy promenade again . . . for the fourth time. Still no sign of Zach. She had a nasty feeling that London in 1871 wouldn't be kind to a boy who was deaf.

TEN

Driven by his excitement that they had time-travelled, Matt darted out into the tide of pedestrians walking north along the Victoria Embankment. Em lunged at her brother, pulling him back under the plank steps.

'Wait,' hissed Em. 'We need to find Zach first. No exploring. We shouldn't leave this general area until we find him.'

'Don't you want to explore a little? That's probably what Zach's doing.'

'You know it's not.'

Matt shrugged. 'Okay. I know. I know.'

Em scanned the busy promenade again for Zach, her eyes on anyone blond, tall and about Zach's age, but her mind kept returning to something else, something more worrying.

'Matt, how will we get back to the Abbey? How will we find Mum if we get trapped in the nineteenth century?'

Matt climbed up on to the Embankment wall for a better view. 'I expect all we have to do is destroy our sketch of the painting and flash, bang, zoom— we'll be home. But I'm not ready to do that.' He looked down at her. 'Are you?'

'Flash, bang, zoom?' She tucked her hair behind her ears, once and then again two more times, a gesture Matt recognized as Em's habit when she was anxious. His mum did the same thing, especially when she was concentrating on her art or thinking about their dad.

Matt smiled at his sister, making her feel a little better. 'You know what I mean.'

'Matt, I appreciate your confidence in our abilities, but I don't care if Queen Victoria and Prince Albert drive past in a carriage; we're not going anywhere or doing anything else until we find Zach.'

'Jeez, Em, you're starting to annoy me again. We'll find him, I promise, but I just want to look around for a minute.'

Em grabbed her brother's wrist and climbed up on to the wall next to him. She squeezed, finding his pulse the way Simon had taught her.

'Mattie, listen to me. You and I are going to find Zach right now. We are not doing anything else. No sightseeing. No wandering off. We're going to find Zach.'

She kept her concentration on his breathing, shifting her calm into his mind, trailing after his thinking, loosening his stubborn feelings from their moorings.

For a few seconds, Em held Matt's thoughts in her head, his excitement frozen, his inclination to dart off weakening. She thought she had calmed him, until he whipped his hand from hers, laughing.

'Seriously, Em, you're trying to inspirit me?'

Em shrugged. 'Worth a try.'

She did her best to mask her delight from his mind. Because despite his protesting, Matt had stopped trying to charge off on his own and was scanning the busy avenue for Zach in a fairly focused way instead.

'I see him,' shouted Matt suddenly. 'He's

40

over there.' He pointed near the railway bridge. 'Somehow he must have fallen from the animation before we did.'

Zach was caught in the middle of a gang of scruffy boys, many of them about the twins' age but a few much younger. Em could sense the volatile emotions of the group. She understood that they were about to pummel poor Zach, who was not so much afraid as confused. It was clear that he was still reeling from the fact that he had fallen into a scene from *Oliver Twist*.

Help!

Finally, Em heard Zach's cries in her head.

Run in the direction of Big Ben, Zach!

Zach dodged the first wharf rat that charged at him and dashed out into the busy avenue. But because he couldn't hear the yelled warning from a pedestrian nearby, he sprinted directly in front of a soldier on a black horse.

The horse bucked and rose up on its hind legs, its front hooves beating the air next to Zach's head. Yanking on the reins with one hand, the soldier swooped down and grabbed Zach's hoodie with his other, pulling a windmilling Zach off his feet and into the air.

The gang of urchins fled in multiple directions, making it difficult for a nearby policeman to catch any of them. The soldier kept a tight grip on Zach's sweatshirt, despite Zach's squirming and kicking to free himself.

Zach, we're coming.

'Got one here for you, constable!'

The piercing pitch of a policeman's whistle rose above the din of the street. Within seconds, a black police wagon trundled out of a cobbled lane next to

Whitehall.

'And here's a lesson for you, you filthy urchin! I'll teach you not to frighten my horse.'

Zach's pain buckled Em to her knees. The soldier had slipped his riding crop from his saddle and begun thrashing Zach, who curled up on the ground, covering his head. Em slid from the wall and howled with every lash of the soldier's riding crop on Zach's back and shoulders. It was all Matt could do not to run to Zach's aid, but he couldn't leave his sister in this state.

'Breathe, Em,' Matt ordered, white with rage for his friend. 'We'll help him. We will. But you need to be calm.'

When the soldier stopped whipping Zach, Em exhaled in a burst of air. Her eyes were red-rimmed. Matt helped her up from the pavement. The twins watched helplessly as Zach was tossed into the prison wagon, already crowded with filthy children, and driven into the flow of traffic heading north towards the dome of St Paul's Cathedral.

ELEVEN

'But where's this prison wagon *going*?' asked Matt, as he and Em raced along the muck-filled gutter of the Embankment in hot pursuit of Zach, dodging round carts, wild dogs and endless people.

'Victorian street children were rounded up and taken to workhouses,' she panted. 'I'm guessing that's where we're going.'

She stopped, her hands on her knees, coughing and breathing hard. It wasn't comfortable running in this thick smog. 'We'll never catch him at this rate. God, this place stinks.' She scraped muck from her shoe and tried to spit the stench from her mouth.

Zach, we're coming. I promise.

'Can you still hear him?' Matt asked.

'Barely.'

Ahead of them, the police wagon was already slipping from their view, rolling round the curve of the riverbank up ahead.

'Give me our drawing,' demanded Em.

'Why?' asked Matt, fishing the page out of the back pocket of his jeans. 'We're not going back without Zach.'

Em smiled at what she was sure was the result of her successful inspiriting. Ducking round three nannies in crisp uniforms pushing prams as big as ponies, she dragged Matt behind a flower-seller's cart and handed him one of the crayons.

43

'What are you thinking?' Matt asked.

'We need to draw something that moves fast.' She glanced down at the river. 'I've got it! Come on.'

Em led Matt down the shaky jetty steps to the river's edge. The stench was worse down here, and Matt's eyes began to water. A rowing boat was beached on the hard, black sand, a fisherman wading by the riverbank.

Em sketched the outline of their animation first. Immediately, Matt discerned what she had in her mind and began to draw with her, sharing the image in their imaginations.

Heads touching, they scribbled across a page of paper so quickly that sparks of light and flakes of colour came popping from the tips of their fingers. A riot of black lines shot upwards, looping, linking, weaving together in the air until a sleek, dark watercraft, a jet ski, appeared on the water in front of them.

Matt jumped on the front before Em could argue and roared the throttle. Em climbed on behind him, gripping him tightly around his waist. The twins bounced out into the tide of vessels on the jet ski, leaving the fisherman watching in stunned disbelief, wondering what terrible plague had seized his brain.

TWELVE

With anxiety twisting in his gut and his shoulders stinging from the soldier's thrashing, Zach watched the twins disappear from his sight through a tear in the thick black curtains that the driver had dropped over the sides of the police wagon, as if something distasteful and disturbing lurked underneath.

He shifted on to his knees and took in his surroundings. He was next to three sleeping children piled one on top of the other like sacks of flour and two boys—at least he *thought* they were boys—who looked no more than seven or eight years old. All the children had a similar look to them. They seemed terribly old.

Underneath the muck that coated each child's body and the matted hair that hung limply against their faces, Zach sensed not fear but resignation and something else—hunger. When he focused his mind on to one of the boys nearest him, Zach also picked up a thin thread of hope that wherever they were going, they would be given something to eat.

Zach's stomach rumbled. Jeannie had made a roast for lunch, which meant thick beef sandwiches and slices of sweet onions from the Abbey's garden would be on the table for supper. Zach looked at the skeletal bodies of the sleeping children pressed next to him and felt guilt for his salivating.

Because Zach had been the last one picked up by the wagon, he was pressed against the door.

He hoped the lock was as rusty on the inside as it looked on the outside.

Zach, we're coming, I promise.

He had only been to London once with his dad a couple of years ago, when they had come down from Scotland to see an exhibition at the Royal Academy, so Zach had no frame of reference for where the bouncing cart was taking him. Slipping his penknife from his pocket, he huddled over the wagon's lock. It would be easier for everyone if he escaped this wheeled cage and met Matt and Em on the road.

He jiggled, turned, and twisted the end of his knife in the lock.

Nothing.

'What you doing?' asked one of the boys crammed next to him.

Zach continued, unaware of the boy addressing him until the boy slapped the knife from Zach's hand and scrambled over the sleeping children to press his filthy face into Zach's. Another boy reached the knife before Zach could retrieve it, tossing it to the first boy, who thrust it against Zach's throat.

'I asked you a question.'

Although he looked younger than Zach, the boy had already lost many of his front teeth. His breath was as foul as the air in the wagon, and his eyes were dead.

Zach grabbed the boy's knife hand and squeezed his wrist.

You don't want to hurt me, Zach projected into the boy's mind. *You're tired and you're so very hungry and you'll feel much better if you ignore me.*

The boy's grip loosened on the knife enough for

Zach to roll away. Quickly, Zach flipped on to his back, pressed his feet against the lock and kicked with all his might. The lock snapped. He tore open the draped tarp and, without thinking about where he was going to end up, he jumped out and into the seething streets of Victorian London.

THIRTEEN

The twins skimmed across the surface of the River Thames on the jet ski, Em's eyes focused on the black-draped wagon labouring above them on the Embankment. Matt was doing his best to dodge in and out of the slow-moving barges and torpedo-shaped steam ships cluttering the river's lanes. Two sailors yelled in astonishment from a barge, and a few tenants of a row of slum housing, lining a section of the Embankment like stacked shoe boxes, yelled for them to stop, but for the most part the twins and their jet ski might have been invisible.

I'm out! I'm heading back towards Big Ben.

Em started at the sound of Zach's voice in her head.

Matt! Zach's out of the wagon. Turn round. He's running back the way he just went.

Communicating telepathically made it easier for the twins to hear each other over the roar of the traffic around them. They could also keep their mouths closed and not have to swallow the stench.

The river was sweating filth.

Matt cut the craft into its own wake, barely missing two punters dressed for a picnic with their colourfully dressed lady friends in wide-brimmed hats. The waves bounced and tipped the spluttering picnickers out of their boats and into the water.

'Sorry,' yelled Em, as the four shocked

Victorians crawled to the safety of the riverbank, their baskets, boats, straw hats and parasols floating away from them in the strong current.

Above them, Zach was sprinting back towards Charing Cross Bridge. Two policemen, looking like extras from a silent film, were in close pursuit, having heard the warning bells of the wagon driver when his vehicle had been emptied of its cargo seconds after Zach tumbled to the street.

Zach spotted a horse-drawn omnibus pulling away from a crowded pedestrian stand. Cutting into the street, he ran, leaping on to the bus platform, bouncing the entire bus as he did so. He scrambled up the circular steps to the top deck. The policemen were still following, and so was the child-catcher in the black wagon.

There's a posse chasing me.

Unfortunately for Zach, the omnibus took on and released passengers regularly. The men chasing him were catching up. At the next stop, he would be trapped.

*   *   *

Em could now see Zach standing at the rear of the bus, watching the chase on the road behind him. Matt darted between two coal barges and shot underneath Charing Cross Bridge as Em clung to his waist.

Matt flung a thought at his twin sister.

Tell Zach to get on the pedestrian side of the bridge. He'll lose them in the crowds up there.

Em stared up at the bridge packed with pedestrians walking across to the east bank of the Thames and a line of sad-looking men and women pushing their overflowing carts along the edges of the bridge. There was hardly any space between them and the rails.

Zach? At the next bus stop, climb off.

But they'll catch me.

Not if you climb on to the struts of the railway bridge.

Matt was doing his best to hold the jet ski steady as they bounced beneath in the waves.

'We can't sit here like rubber ducks for long, Em,' he yelled. 'It's too dangerous. We'll be spotted.'

'I've got an idea,' said Em, patting their sketch of Monet's painting tucked away in her pocket. 'But Zach needs to get off that bus. And fast.'

FOURTEEN

At Charing Cross Station, the mail sacks had been loaded on to the train. Leaning from his carriage, the conductor whistled his signal to the driver in the engine at the front. The driver signalled the engineer, who fired up the boiler.

A belch of black smoke followed by coughs of white steam erupted from the funnel, filling the station. The train's pistons gasped and wheezed, its iron limbs spewing steam, chugging the train from the station, gathering speed as it emerged into the daylight, on to the bridge and over the River Thames.

*   *   *

Zach waited until most of the passengers had climbed down from the top deck of the omnibus before he jumped, scraping his arms and legs as he landed on the struts of the railway bridge.

You need to get to the footbridge fast, Zach. If the police climb to the top of the bus, they'll see you. When you've made it, jump over and into the river. We'll tear up the sketch as you're falling and get us all out of here.

That's your best plan?

Zach's terror jarred Em's mind.

Trust me.

'Aw, man,' said Matt, shifting the jet ski closer to

51

the bridge.

An official-looking tug boat was steaming towards them.

'What are we going to do?' asked Matt, panicking.

'Try to keep us steady for a few more minutes,' said Em. Her heart was pounding at the audacity of what they were trying to do.

Zach had climbed the struts of the bridge and disappeared. Em could no longer see him.

She could hear the train whistle as it thundered into view, looking like an iron monster belching black smoke and white steam. The men chasing Zach were on the top of the bus, pointing and shouting.

Em followed their gestures. Her heart froze. Zach had made a mistake. Instead of dropping down on to the footbridge, he had ended up on the train tracks. She could see him desperately trying to find a way off. The locomotive was charging at him, its bells and whistles screaming, the bridge vibrating with its weight and speed.

'Matt!' Em screamed. 'Zach's on the tracks!'

On the bridge, Zach felt the locomotive before he saw its massive face rising up out of the steam on the crest of the bridge.

Climb over the side and jump! Now, Zach!

The train was charging closer. Zach's heart was racing and his mouth was dry. Tears were gathering in his eyes, blurring his vision. He felt sick. He was going to die, and his dad would never know what had happened to him.

This isn't going to work, Em. The train's too fast and the steam is going to burn me alive.

Matt steadied the jet ski directly under Zach's

tiny figure on the bridge. Em was crying, feeling Zach's terror. Behind the twins, the tug boat was almost upon them.

Jump, Zach!

You're out of your mind! We'll all die if I land on top of you.

We're not going to let you hit us. Matt thinks if we tear up the sketch as soon as you get close, we'll be okay.

Matt THINKS? This is so not a great plan, Em!

'Jump!' screamed Matt, even though he knew Zach couldn't hear him.

'Oh no! No!' screamed Em in horror. 'The train's going to hit him! It's too late!' *Jump!*

The engine was bearing down on Zach, a black beast spewing fire. And Zach was swallowed up in clouds of hissing steam and choking black smoke, the sounds of Em's cries filling his head.

PART TWO

FIFTEEN

The Monastery of Era Mina
Middle Ages

After taking his leave of Brother Renard, Cornelius and the Abbot, Solon made his way down to the water's edge. Dusk was falling, and as if someone had already summoned it, the peryton was waiting on the shore, its wings folded back against its haunches, its silvery antlers and lustrous coat shimmering like crushed velvet and illuminating the spot with its enchanted brilliance. At the sound of Solon approaching, the beast lifted its head and stretched to its full height.

Solon held out his hand in greeting. The beast trotted forward, bending its forelegs and tilting its antlers to meet Solon's careful caress.

'Greetings, my friend,' said Solon, stroking the stag's thick neck, feeling a warmth radiating up his arm and into his chest.

Suddenly, despite the task ahead, Solon's whole being filled with confidence, the fears he had about entering Skinner's Bog diminishing in his mind. He felt the way he did when the Abbot calmed him.

Had the peryton the power to inspirit?

Solon climbed on to the peryton's back. With graceful ease, the creature rose up into the moonlit sky, its gleaming white presence gliding over the tall trees and looking to the curious villagers below like a swift silver cloud. The peryton's wingspan was wider than the spreading branches of the greatest tree in the forest, and yet it flew with only a faint whoosh of its wings.

Solon peered down in wonder as the monastery and Brother Renard's partly-built tower on the northern tip of Era Mina sank away beneath him. From this vantage point, he could see the islands in their entirety for the first time. He marvelled at how tranquil they looked.

Shifting forward, Solon gripped the peryton's neck.

'You need not worry about navigating to the bog,' the Abbot had told him. 'The peryton will find the place.'

A rough journey that would have taken Solon hours on foot had taken only moments. The silvery white peryton landed between two tall pines, the feathered tips of its wings grazing the branches and leaving a patina of white on the leaves like a dusting of snow. Kneeling on its front legs, the peryton let Solon slide on to the crunchy undergrowth that littered the forest floor. Skinner's Bog was directly ahead of him. He'd seen it from above.

For a moment, Solon stood with his back to the peryton, getting his bearings. He felt small and vulnerable in the creature's company, but sensed no threat from the magnificent beast— only a buzzing heat from its body. The peryton had brought him to the centre of Auchinmurn, beside the island's highest peak, riddled with caves and treacherous pitched overhangs that had seen many a robber or smuggler wandering in the dark and falling over the edge to the jagged rocks below.

Solon crouched and picked up a handful of pine-needles. There was no scent, no perfume from the pine, no suggestion of the wild mint that Solon knew was everywhere on these islands. This was the most isolated place he had ever been.

The wind was still, the stars bright. But beneath the canopy of the tall pines and oaks, they contributed very little light. In the glow from the peryton, Solon took a few steps towards the Devil's Dyke—a ring of monolithic standing stones that formed a barrier round the bog. The villagers on Auchinmurn and many of the monks believed the Devil and his minions had erected this megalith to protect the bog's secrets. Legend told that only the Devil himself, riding on his black stag, could pass through the stones and the impenetrable undergrowth beyond.

Solon leaped out of his skin as he heard the sound of grass being torn up somewhere to his left, before realizing that it was only wild sheep grazing nearby. He felt a change in the air around him. The darkness was heavy, as if it had a presence. Up this high, the night was tangible. A sheen of sweat settled beneath his leather tunic and leggings. The gloom felt as if it was seeping under his garments and crawling along his skin.

He rubbed his arms together. It was cold. In the darkness, he could barely make out the thick swirling outlines of nettles and hawthorn bushes crowded together beyond the stones, their leaves glistening in the pale starlight.

The peryton stood to its full height, startling Solon from his reverie. Its eyes blazed with a light so strong that it illuminated everything. Solon stared at the brightly lit thorny briars and nettles

59

surrounding the obelisks before him. How was he ever going to get through that tangled mass?

The peryton pounded its hoofs on the ground and raised its wings high into the air. But the creature did not lift up into the heavens. Instead, Solon had to jump out of its path as it trotted forward, the light radiating from its body revealing a narrow opening through the jagged thorns that Solon would swear had not been there a moment ago.

The peryton had created a path for him.

Solon inched forward. When he reached the opening in the thorn bushes, he placed his hand on the peryton's flank with his heart pounding in his own ears. Creature and boy walked together into the narrow gap, the darkness a weight on Solon's head and shoulders.

SIXTEEN

The landscape changed in an instant, the ground softening and the air thickening. When Solon felt the dry undergrowth shift to swamp under his feet, he noticed that the peryton was no longer next to him. The creature had stopped at the perimeter of the bog, holding its head high and keeping a blanket of light on the desolate landscape.

Stepping out of the twisted brambles, Solon suddenly plunged to his knees into the putrid muck of Skinner's Bog. His leggings caked with thick black silt, Solon felt himself being pulled into complete darkness. He could no longer see the peryton, or its light. Terrified, he turned around. More darkness.

Panic and bile bubbled in his gut. Then he saw the light, and sensed the peryton's steadfastness. It was helping him, projecting its strength to him.

Solon touched the leather pouch fastened round his waist and took two more steps forward. He had to keep his bearings. If he could make it to the centre of the bog and find the rowan tree, Brother Cornelius would be able to heal those who were still suffering.

That way, he thought, shifting a little to his left.

But then he stopped. To go in that direction would take him away from the centre.

It was so dark that Solon couldn't tell any more which way was forward. The peryton calmed the young novice, suffusing him with a fresh wave of understanding. Now Solon knew that he had to move to his right.

Each lunging step he took drained Solon's will to continue. But the peryton's light filled his mind and buoyed him to take the next step, and the next. The darkness had become so heavy that the boy was hunching over as he walked.

A gust of fetid air and a long, low howl suddenly blasted Solon on to his back. He could feel himself sinking, his arms and legs being sucked into the bog. Hauling himself out of the muck, he focused on the horrible howling. It was impossible to fix the direction it was coming from.

His breath caught in his throat as a shadow rose out of the darkness in front of him. Not a bear, but close in shape and size, with red-hot slits for eyes. The creature was oozing from every part of its body, dark essence dripping to the bog like tar. And the *smell*. It was as if someone had desecrated a grave.

Solon wanted to run, but his feet were stuck. He wanted to yell, but his voice was frozen in his throat.

There was the sound of a splash at the edge of the bog. The Grendel turned its burning eyes away from Solon, the sound distracting its attention. The boy trembled as the monster's feral howling changed to a snapping of jaws: slobbering, slurping, chewing. The howling began again, but from deeper in the bog now.

Solon forced himself to move. Brother Cornelius was depending on him to return.

Solon had taken two more steps forward when something heavy and wet hit his hand. Lunging sideways, Solon saw the bloodied carcass of a sheep. In a moment of sickening awareness, he realized that the sheep had saved his life.

Solon shivered at the sight of the massive jaw marks visible on the flayed animal's neck. In a moment of grim humour, he realized that when he returned to the monastery, he would no longer need to ask the Abbot how Skinner's Bog got its name.

SEVENTEEN

Solon was almost ready to give up and return without the precious berries from the rowan tree. He was cold and scared and tired. Because of the lid of darkness on the bog, he could no longer tell how long he had been tramping through this muck. Every step sucked in his legs deeper than before.

The chewing, slobbering noises were everywhere in the dark.

At long last he reached the grassy mound at the centre—and the rowan tree. Solon pushed his matted hair off his face to get a clearer look at his prize. Caught in a ribbon of the palest starlight, the tree looked dressed for a royal ball, its berries glowing like millions of tiny red lanterns. The tree reminded Solon of the ones that Brother Renard had used to illustrate initials in his manuscripts.

But it was the boy curled beneath the tree that took Solon's breath away.

He stumbled on to the grassy mound before the Grendel decided to feed again. The peryton might have sacrificed the sheep to the Grendel, but Solon didn't think the trick would work a second time. He had to hurry. As soon as he stepped on to the grassy mound, the weight of the darkness lifted from Solon's shoulders, and the terrible gnawing noises of the Grendel quieted.

Solon supposed from the boy's size that he was about his own age: fifteen or so. Wrapped in a blue wool cloak with only his fur boots showing, the boy was tucked tight against the trunk of the rowan. Sleeping, Solon guessed. Darting forward, he rolled the boy on to his back—and gasped again.

It was a girl. A Viking girl no less, by her ruddy complexion, her long, white-blonde hair and the detailing on her cloak pin. She was lying in an awkward position. Solon thought she looked broken.

The girl wasn't asleep. She was wounded. A wide gash above her elbow was oozing a soupy pus from the frayed edges of its cloth wrapping. The wrapping was soaked in what, at first glance, looked like blood.

Other than his sisters, Solon had had no contact with girls. This one obviously knew about the rowan tree's powers, because it wasn't blood on the cloth—it was a poultice made from rowan berries, the crushed fruit pressing on to her raw wound.

How had she got here? Had she been left behind by the invaders? *That was nonsense*, thought Solon. Viking bands didn't travel with women, never mind girls of fifteen. Perhaps she was a Viking slave? Or perhaps she was a trick of the swamp, a fairy spirit who would stop Solon from taking berries from the tree.

He quickly filled his pouch with as much of the rowan fruit as he could.

Then the girl cried softly. Solon flinched at the memories that he could suddenly see in her mind: the screaming of the monks, the crying of village children, the killer gleam in the Vikings' eyes. Solon saw the cobbles of the Abbey running red with blood—a blow with an axe from one of the Auchinmurn villagers and the white-hot agony of the wound the moment it had occurred. He leaned to one side and retched at the pain.

Wiping his mouth, Solon hesitated, unsure of what he should do next.

The girl moaned again. She looked half-dead. Solon decided that, friend or foe, she needed his help.

Lifting his water pouch from over his shoulder, Solon gently dribbled the liquid on to her pale lips. His hands were shaking, and most of the water sloshed on to her face.

Her eyes popped open. If it hadn't been for the glint of the knife's hilt and Solon's quick reflexes, he would have lost an ear.

'Trying to drown me?' she asked, coughing out the words in a language that Solon recognized as Norse. Keeping the knife under Solon's chin, she struggled to use her injured arm to lift herself up against the tree. What little colour she had in her cheeks immediately drained away.

If you stop threatening me, you stupid girl, I might be able to help you, Solon thought irritably.

I don't need your help, you stupid boy!

EIGHTEEN

The Abbey
Present Day

As he charged into the sitting room, Simon knew immediately that the twins had animated themselves into a painting. Luminous flecks of white, ochre and blue floated in the air near the easel like hundreds of fireflies.

Simon spotted Zach's laptop sitting on the couch. Setting his palm on it, he felt the warmth from its battery and the surge of his son's conflicted emotions while he'd been working on the computer.

At least he tried to stop them, thought Simon.

'Those weans are nowhere to be found,' said Jeannie, following Simon into the sitting room. Taking off the reflective orange safety vest that she wore when she was near the water's edge, she added, 'I even checked the boathouse. Not a sign of them.'

'They've not been gone long. Zach's laptop's still warm,' said Simon. 'And I'm afraid I know where they are.'

He nodded towards the painting perched on the easel. Jeannie's hand went up to her mouth. 'No! They would'nae dare.'

'No doubt about it, that painting's been animated,' said Simon. 'I should've known better than to leave them alone. Matt's been champing at the bit to get out of here for days.'

'Aye,' Jeannie sighed, 'he's been taking it hard that he and Em can't go tearing around the country to search for their mother.'

Simon picked up a copy of Em's drawing of the peryton. 'Em's been doing some good work, hasn't she? This sketch feels alive. Look at the depth in the beast's wings.' He set the drawing down again absently. 'Wherever they are, Zach's with them.'

'Well, he would be, wouldn't he,' said Jeannie, a knowing smile loosening the worry in her expression for a moment. 'Especially if Em went along, too. He never lets the lass out of his sight for long.'

'They've gone into a painting.' Renard Calder, the twin's grandfather and one of the most powerful Guardians in the world, had entered the sitting room and instantly recoiled as if touched by an electric shock. Like Simon, Renard could see and feel the fireflies of colour and light, the residual energy of the twins' animation.

'Monet's *Thames below Westminster*,' said Simon, nodding as if at a question Renard had not asked.

'Ah, one of Monet's first London paintings,' said Renard, recovering. 'Claude himself gave it to my great-grandfather in return for a room near the Thames with lots of English sunlight.'

'Was there ever such a thing?' enquired Jeannie. 'English sunlight, I mean.'

'I'm not surprised they picked this one,' said Simon. 'Matt's been more homesick than usual these past few days.'

'Poor lad, he misses London terribly,' said

68

Jeannie, folding her safety vest over the back of a chair before dropping into it.

'Well, he won't be seeing the real city again for quite some time,' said Renard. 'It's still too dangerous. The Council of Guardians will bind the children for sure once they're sixteen if they keep animating into paintings. It breaks every rule in the book.'

Jeannie looked terrified at the thought of the twins being bound.

Simon watched the brilliant shards of colour twinkling like stars above Monet's painting. A flash of foreboding blackened his thoughts. He couldn't smother his dread that something big and bad was coming into their lives.

The shards of light and colour surrounding the Monet suddenly began inflating to the size of balloons, almost blinding the three adults with their brilliance. For a brief moment, Simon saw a cresting wave. Worse than that, he could hear Em sobbing.

Jeannie cried out. Renard struggled off the couch. As quickly as the energy from the animation had expanded, the colourful orbs shrank back to a million slivers of confetti.

'After a burst of animation like that,' said Renard sharply, 'I'd have expected the children to have fallen out of the painting.'

'Something's wrong,' burst out Simon. The children's fear was still twisting behind his temples. 'The strength of this animation doesn't make sense. What can possibly be that bad inside such a tranquil Impressionist painting, for God's sake?'

'Whatever's happening, I'm sure they will find a way out of it,' said Renard as reassuringly as he could. 'We've underestimated the twins' powers before.'

Much as I underestimated their father's. The words hung unspoken in the air.

NINETEEN

Skinner's Bog
Auchinmurn Isle
Middle Ages

Solon was dumbfounded to hear the Viking girl's voice sniping in his head. An unfortunate reaction that served to reinforce the girl's impression of his stupidity.

His skin was tingling, his pulse quickening, and his throat felt as if he was swallowing sawdust. In a nervous rush, he returned to jamming his pouch with rowan berries, even stuffing a few sprigs into the pockets of his leather tunic like a madman.

What is your name?

'Solon,' he replied out loud, cautiously.

Since arriving at the monastery, the only other person Solon had been able to hear clearly in his head was Brother Renard. He had always assumed that this was on account of Brother Renard's abilities and the relationship they had as master and novice.

'Solon,' she said, nodding.

The exertion of pulling up against the tree had opened the wound on her arm again. Solon reached out to help, but she pushed him away and, with more difficulty, stood up. She was too unsteady on her feet. Solon caught her before she fell against the sharp branches of the tree or,

71

worse, face first into the muck of Skinner's Bog.

'And your name?' he asked, quickly releasing her from his arms. Would she be able to understand his question?

'I am called Carik Grimsdóttir,' she replied. She sensed Solon's puzzlement. 'My mother taught me your language. She once lived on this land.'

'Was your mother captured? Taken during a raid?'

Solon was about to speak again when she put her fingers to her lips to silence him. The darkness over the bog was thickening, the smell of rotting flesh once more rising from the muck.

'The creature is returning. I can hear it,' she said.

'Was it the creature who injured you?'

She nodded. Solon could hear only his and Carik's breathing. They stood in silence for a moment.

'We need to leave this bog,' said Solon, taking a step out into the knee-deep muck. 'The monks have great powers. They will be able to heal you.'

'But I am your enemy,' she said, surprised.

Solon looked at the beautiful girl staring back at him. 'You're not my enemy.'

Without warning, Carik lunged at Solon, pulling him back and out of the bog. Solon flinched as he heard the horrible sucking sounds, the same noises he had heard earlier in the dark. The Grendel was almost upon them. Its low growls carried in a cold wind that cut across the grassy mound, bending the branches of the rowan tree to the ground. The blackness had become a heavy canopy.

We are trapped, Solon. How could one beast surround us?

That's the nature of the Grendel, answered Solon, so naturally that he surprised himself. *It is made of the blackness that's only found beyond death.*

A guzzling noise shattered the darkness in front of them. The Grendel, the mud-monster, the spirit-stalker, rose up out of the bog in a swirling tornado of foul mud and flaming red eyes.

Its body was made up of layers of wet clay, as if it had been formed on a potter's wheel deep under the bog, and it had no front or hind legs—only a shapeless form trailing behind it, devouring vegetation and sucking up everything in its wake.

The Grendel's head rose higher and higher out of the bog, expanding until it was more massive than the ground on which Solon and Carik were cowering.

Carik unsheathed her dagger, flipped her cape behind her shoulders, raised her head and prepared to battle the beast. Solon knew she must be terrified and in awful pain, yet he could feel an unswerving calm emanating from her. Carik's strength fed his imagination.

Tearing a piece of bark from the rowan tree, Solon grabbed Carik's hand, squashing a handful of berries into her fist. He used his own knife to sharpen the end of a stick. Dipping the point of the stick into the viscous red juice cupped in Carik's hand, Solon closed his eyes and let his imagination draw.

Closer and closer, the Grendel's massive jaws ground through the crushing blackness.

TWENTY

Although Solon had never left the Western Isles of Scotland, he had travelled far and had seen many wonderful things through the monastery's books. And one of those wonders was a Roman general's manuscript, describing and illustrating the weapons of a castle siege.

Solon let his fingers fly across the bark, trying to replicate the weapon he had in his mind. When he finished the drawing, his heart sank. Nothing had happened. He was too young and untrained to animate yet on his own. The terrible stench from the monster was suffocating, its jaws opening and closing as if already tasting its prey.

'Move!' yelled Carik, shoving Solon against the rowan tree, as a blinding flash of light burst from the bark. On the spot where Solon had been drawing, a colossal catapult—a trebuchet with a bucket as big as a wagon—appeared between them. Light sparked from its wooden wheels and a woven red canopy covered it. Solon's heart leaped with pride and wonder to see what he had created.

Above them, the mud-monster widened its mouth, releasing a gust of fetid air that dropped Carik and Solon to their knees in disgust.

'HROOOO!'

The Grendel's eyes caught Solon in their sight, the monster's gaze burning his skin. It slid forward, muck oozing from its clay-like shell. Any moment

74

now, its jaws would sink down over Solon and swallow him whole.

Release the handles, Carik!

Carik threw herself against the double wooden handles of the trebuchet. They popped and wheezed like oversized bellows, released the spring and catapulted lethal quicksilver directly on top of the Grendel.

The burning mercury seeped through the Grendel's scaly layers, scorching through the filth to the centre of the beast. The Grendel seemed to melt, screaming and dissolving into the depths of Skinner's Bog.

Solon and Carik stood under the rowan tree and stared at each other. Carik's expression was a mingling of awe and fear.

'You are one who draws? An Animare?'

Carik pronounced it in such a way that Solon thought it sounded even more magical.

He nodded.

'I thought so when I first saw you.'

Avoiding Carik's eyes, Solon secured his pouch more tightly round his waist, making sure it still held the rowan berries. A faint glow was pulsing in the distance beyond the bog. He hoped it was the peryton.

Solon's apprenticeship had not prepared him for this kind of situation. He put out his hand. 'We should go,' he said awkwardly. 'I don't know what forces brought the Grendel out to hunt, but I don't want to stay here and find out.'

She laughed, ignored his hand and set off across the bog by herself, being careful to avoid the place where the Grendel had sunk from view. Solon followed.

Slogging through the thick mud was difficult enough for the uninjured young monk. For Carik, with her shoulder wound bleeding again and pain slowing her, it was close to impossible. At the far edge of the bog, Solon pulled Carik from the treacherous muck. This time she offered him very little resistance.

The gleam from the peryton grew stronger, guiding them. As they hobbled towards the soft light, the mud in the bog behind them began to bubble angrily. A monstrous cloud of foul air skirted across the surface of the bog and trailed after them.

'Time to run!' Solon advised breathlessly. 'If you can!'

They scrambled through the gap in the briars as fast as they could. The peryton was on its haunches and ready for them. Carik gasped at the sight of such a magnificent beast, but was too weak and in too much pain to say a word. She collapsed at its feet.

The peryton dropped as close to the ground as it could, and Solon reached under Carik and gently lifted her on to its back. Then he climbed on behind her, making sure she was as comfortable as possible. Carik's head flopped forward on to the peryton's neck, as the creature bounded gracefully along the rocky hillside and soared into the air.

Carik suddenly shifted, tipping off to the side. Frantically, Solon steadied her, gripping her even more tightly, doing his best to ignore the softness of the pale skin on her neck, as the peryton pitched into a gentle turn towards the monastery.

TWENTY-ONE

The Abbey
Present Day

Matt and Em fell out of Monet's painting in a rush of foul air and a torpedo of dense grey light, hitting the cluttered art table full on and collapsing it under their weight with a thunderous crash. Less than a second behind them, Zach hurtled out on top of the twins, his elbow jabbing Matt hard in the eye.

'Ow!' yelled Matt, shoving Zach on to the floor.

Shut up! You'll wake everyone, Em telepathed to both boys.

The sitting room was pitch black, the heavy curtains drawn across all the windows. *11:19* was flashing on the Blu-ray. They'd been gone for roughly two hours.

Em crawled over to Zach, who was on his stomach on the floor, catching his breath. His heart was racing, and every nerve in his body was wired.

That was too close, Em. I felt the heat from that engine.

'I told you my plan would work,' said Matt.

'We were lucky,' replied Em, climbing off the collapsed table. 'One second more and we'd all be . . .' *Are you okay, Zach?*

Not sure. I feel like that soldier AND that train hit me.

77

Pulling up Zach's T-shirt and hoodie, Em gently touched his back. She felt raw, pink welts criss-crossing his skin; a couple felt as though they were bleeding.

How bad is it, Em?

Bad. We can cover them up in the morning. But we all need showers first. If we go to bed smelling like this, we'll never be able to hide what we've done from Jeannie.

'I'm not okay either, by the way,' said Matt. 'Thanks for asking.'

Em stroked her brother's cheek and rapidly bruising eye. *Poor baby. I'll get some ice.*

Suddenly, the sitting-room lights burst on, blinding the three of them. Simon was looming over the crushed table, hands on his hips. He let loose a current of barbed energy at them.

'You are so busted,' he growled.

Em knew they were in trouble. But the moment she spotted her grandfather sitting on the couch she didn't care. Scrambling up off the floor, she threw herself into Renard's arms.

'I'm so glad you're home from the hospital!' she said in delight.

'And I could say the same about you,' said Renard, squeezing Em tightly, 'but my word, you smell awful.'

'Why didn't anyone tell us you were coming back tonight?' Em asked.

'Would it have mattered if we had?' said Simon, angrily pulling Matt and Zach up from the floor.

'Maybe,' said Matt. 'It would at least have given us something to look forward to other than what's on the stupid menu for dinner.'

Jeannie had heard the thunderous commotion

on her way up the stairs. She rushed into the room, ignored the broken furniture and swooped Em and the boys up in her embrace. Then she caught their stink and threw her hands in the air.

'You all stink like you've been rolling in horse dung!'

Simon suddenly cried out and put his hands to his temples. Renard did the same. His tea cup, which had been balancing on a plate of crumbs, tipped on to the floor.

'Where have you three *been*?' Jeannie went on.

Em could tell that both Simon and Renard had just sensed a wave of extreme energy. The kind of energy Guardians feel when their Animare are animating. But before Em had time to think this through, Matt's thoughts crashed into her head.

Don't tell them we time-travelled.

Em was getting really tired of her brother telling her what to do.

She sat down on the couch and looked at her grandfather. The words exploded from her. 'We went into the Monet for fun, to be in London again for a few minutes. And then we discovered we were actually in London at the same time as Monet when he painted the scene, rather than just being in the painting. But Zach got separated from us when we were animating—we're not sure how—and then he got arrested. Oh, and right before that a soldier on a horse whipped his back. It looks pretty bad.'

Jeannie was staring at the three of them in shock. Em charged on, trying to ignore the way Simon had dropped on to the comfy chair with his head between his legs like he was about to pass out. Her grandfather was as pale as porridge.

'Then a child-catcher threw Zach into his wagon,

79

but Zach managed to escape, which meant that Matt and I were able to find him.'

'You animated into the nineteenth century through this painting?' asked Renard.

'Yes,' said Matt reluctantly. He felt the jolt of alarm pass among the adults. 'I think there must be something in the way our abilities react together.'

'You think? You *think*?' Simon shouted.

Simon seemed more angry about this than Matt thought it warranted.

I don't get why he's so upset, Em.

Well, we did almost get his son killed.

Zach can take care of himself. His dad needs to realize that.

Maybe, but we put him in danger.

Zach came along with us willingly. Remember?

'Have you done this before?' Simon asked. Renard appeared lost in his own thoughts. 'The truth!'

'No!' said Em.

She felt the way she had when she and Matt had first arrived at the island, wanting to impress Renard and Simon. To show them that she, Matt and their special talents were worth caring about.

'Wait a wee minute there, young man!' said Jeannie suddenly, stepping in front of Matt and placing her hands on his chest as he was about to sit next to Em. 'Don't you dare sit yourself on that couch stinking like my grandfather's auld bothie.'

'But Em's sitting,' said Matt. Exhaustion was settling over his mind and his body with a weight he'd never felt before. He guessed that animating to another century had physical consequences.

'Jeannie's right,' said Simon. 'Showers and wounds cleaned.' He took a quick look at his son's back and flinched. 'Get to your rooms, now.'

TWENTY-TWO

Teenagers and adults all gathered in the hallway of the children's wing of the Abbey. The sitting room separated Em's and Matt's bedrooms. Zach's was next to Matt's, and the boys shared a bathroom. Em, as the only girl, had a bedroom with an en-suite bathroom.

'Can you remember anything else about the night Mum disappeared, Grandpa?' asked Em, walking Renard to the stairs. 'Anything?'

'Nothing, Em,' Renard replied. 'I'm sorry.'

Behind them, Em could hear Simon still grilling the boys, while Jeannie dashed down to the kitchen to get the first-aid kit for Zach's wounds. Em sighed, knowing the dressing-down would come her way sooner or later.

Her grandfather's suite was in the south tower of the Abbey, which meant he had to go downstairs, across the foyer and along the hallway to reach his room. Renard lifted Em on to her toes on the edge of the stairs, giving her a fierce bear-hug.

'We'll discuss what you and your brother have done more fully in the morning.' Looking deep into Em's eyes, he added, 'Please . . . please stay put until then. Promise me?'

'I will,' she said, kissing his forehead. She was aware that when she snuggled under the duvet on her bed, she would sleep like a log, exhausted and glad to be back in the twenty-first century.

Halfway down the stairs, Renard stopped, staring up at a still-life painting on the wall above him.

'Is this a new piece?' he asked.

'Hasn't it always been there?' said Em.

One of the things that the twins had first noticed when they arrived at the Abbey was that every wall in every room was covered in paintings of every artistic style and historical period. If there wasn't a window on a wall, there were paintings.

The still-life in question showed a primitive writing desk with carved legs and one narrow drawer. On the surface of the desk sat a brass candelabra with two burning candles of similar lengths, a skull with a gaping hole for a mouth and a pewter goblet tipped on its side on a piece of mirrored glass. Zach and Matt leaned over the upstairs banisters as Simon joined Renard on the stairs to look more closely at the painting.

'Are ye all waiting for a parade out here?' Jeannie asked, coming across the landing from the kitchen staircase with the first-aid kit. 'Mr R, this is enough for one night. These weans should get cleaned up and be off to bed.'

'Grandpa's curious about this painting,' said Matt. 'Did you hang it here, Jeannie?'

Jeannie passed Simon the lotion for Zach's back and handed an ice-pack to Matt for his eye, before glancing at the painting. 'It looks like any number of still-lifes we have all over the Abbey.'

Simon looked at the date on the gilded frame. 'This says 1848. Must have been one of your great-grandfather's acquisitions, Renard.'

Jeannie took her reading glasses from her pocket, slipped them on and peered at the painting more carefully. 'You know Mr R,' she said after a moment, 'even after a blow to yer head, when you're right, you're right.'

'What?' the twins asked in unison.

'That's one of the Abbey's pewter goblets sitting on that old desk,' said Jeannie, pointing at the goblet with the arm of her glasses before returning them to her pocket.

'Maybe the painting was done here at the Abbey,' said Em.

'No, lass, that's not what I meant. I bought six of those goblets in Glasgow last Christmas. How did one of them get into a still-life painted more than one hundred and sixty years ago?'

TWENTY-THREE

The Monastery of Era Mina
Middle Ages

The Abbot sat alone in his study atop the west tower of the monastery. He had not slept since Solon took flight on the peryton over the island towards Skinner's Bog, and his burdens weighed on him like a suit of armour. His worries about old Brother Renard had been overthrown by his fears for the island, and the dark secrets that seemed to be revealing themselves more with each passing day.

He tapped the first page of the unfinished *Book of Beasts* with his fingers. He had removed it from the scriptorium, in a bid to help him think more clearly about the problem before him.

The illuminations shone in the gloom. It was Brother Renard's finest and most profound work, the Abbot had to admit: a sacred legacy for the Order of Era Mina and a gift for all of mankind— the corralling of the beasts of an uncivilized time in one mystical place.

But the bestiary had to be completed. An unfinished manuscript would leave the world in peril. Incomplete, the manuscript could be used to reverse all of Brother Renard's vital work. The Abbot worried that the Order of Era Mina—that Brother Renard himself—would not survive long enough to see this mission fulfilled. *The Book of Beasts* had to be finished, and then buried deep inside the island with its secrets sealed for ever. It was inestimably important.

The Abbot leaned back in his chair, rubbing his hands over his tired eyes. His skin was leathery, even to his own touch.

I'm getting old, he thought, *and still with so much left to accomplish.*

That evening after Vespers, the Abbot had intervened as the monks, some of them still struggling with their injuries from the bloody Viking attack, had protested loudly about the imprudence of not giving the Viking chief what he had wanted. They couldn't endure another attack like this one, should he choose to return with fresh demands. They simply didn't have the numbers.

'With all due respect, Father,' Brother Cornelius had said, 'we should have given the relic to the Norsemen. It means nothing without the book, and both mean nothing without the islands.'

The Abbot's voice had boomed out across the chapel, echoing in the side chapels filled with statues, bouncing off the stone floor.

'My brothers in faith and imagination, we *cannot* return the bone quill to the Norsemen. It is the only remaining relic from the creation of our islands. Our martyred forefathers, who gave their lives to retrieve and protect it, are owed our steadfastness. Even in the face of terrible danger.

'The bone quill is ours to defend, like the island itself. It must remain here at all costs. Let me repeat with no lesser emphasis: the bone quill and *The Book of Beasts* must be protected *at all costs*.'

Sitting at his desk, reflecting on the evening's

draining events, the Abbot knew that he hadn't quelled the brothers' fears and dissatisfaction. Who knew what might happen during the next Viking invasion, or attack from the powerful northern clans, or the Sassenach tribes further south?

These were desperate, dangerous times.

TWENTY-FOUR

'A long time ago, when the world believed monsters roamed the earth,' said Brother Renard, his eyes holding his apprentice's gaze with such intensity that Solon's toes curled against the soles of his sealskin boots, 'a young boy had a strange and beautiful dream.'

Solon had come to Brother Renard's cell first thing that morning to let him know he had returned from his quest unharmed, although with a new-found respect for the monster that lurked in the bog. Brother Cornelius had taken a weakened Carik under his wing, locking her for safety in Brother Renard's old cell with promises to tend to her.

Solon had also told Brother Renard about their terrible confrontation with the Grendel and the peryton's role in their escape. The effect on the old monk was like lightning. He had launched into this tale with more vigour than he had shown since the Viking attack.

'Hush, Brother,' said Solon, worried. 'You are tiring yourself.'

'You must hear this, Solon, my boy. You must. I cannot leave this life until *The Book of Beasts* is finished. The Grendel is the last beast to be locked into that book before I depart this earthly world. Heed this story before my strength fails completely.

'The boy dreamed that two giant stags, one

87

black as the coal deep inside the earth and one as white as the snow that capped its peaks, shattered through a mountain top on the wild Scottish coast,' the old Animare continued. 'First their colossal antlers cracked open the summit, tearing up the very core of the hillside.'

Brother Renard jumped from his chair and raised his hands above his head, mimicking the massive antlers of the stags. Solon's eyes widened, afraid that a pair of antlers would burst through the wrinkled skin of the old monk's head. To his great relief, they did not.

The old monk dropped back to his seat, gripping his hands together once again on his lap.

'The presence of two giant stags on the mountain sent a great avalanche of rock thundering down into the sea. Standing on the craggy summit, the giant stags sloughed off the mountain's debris, stamping their hooves with such might that the mountain cracked in two.'

The shutters on the only window of the tower room clapped noisily. The wind howled through the slits. Solon braced himself, preparing for sharp rocks to slide in through the rattling windows. Thunder erupted above his head, resounding across the thick wooden beams. Solon put his hands over his head as splinters showered down from the ceiling. He shook a splinter of wood from his shaggy blond hair. 'Please, master, go on.'

'When the mountain split its core, it separated into two islands—one large and one small. The force of the rupture also separated the stags, leaving the white one on the bigger island staring longingly at the black stag on the smaller one, across a great and treacherous divide.

'With their antlers shining like polished gems, the two beasts stood at the summit of each island and wept at their division. Their tears became a tidal wave that crashed on to the land, filling the crevices and rocky fissures with water, creating bays and channels and secret coves.'

Brother Renard moved his hands restlessly. Solon knew that he was picturing the unfinished *Book of Beasts* lying in his lap.

'According to our sacred teachings, the white stag could stand its loneliness no longer. It wanted to reunite with its twin. Unfolding a pair of great silver wings, it rose close to the heavens and swooped across the divide.'

'The peryton?' asked Solon.

The old monk nodded. 'Unfortunately, the black stag had grown bitter that it had landed on the smaller island. It did not want to share, especially with such a powerful beast as its twin. When the silver-winged stag landed, the black stag charged.

'The battle raged for an age. Finally, exhausted and with its strength dwindling, the white stag did the one thing it had dared not do before. Under cover of the darkest night, the white stag lifted itself above the black stag, smashing the black stag's antlers and splintering the pieces across the world. Then it lifted its twin into the air and carried both of them far away from the two islands.

'The white stag carried the black one deep into the cold lands of the north, flying until webs of ice laced across its wings. When the ice thickened like leather, it could no longer hold on to its twin. The massive bulk of the black stag fell from the sky to the land of frozen mountains and ice castles.'

TWENTY-FIVE

Solon reached for the jug of warm perry by the fire, made with pears from the monastery orchard. Carefully, he poured two cups: one for the old monk and one for himself.

'Did the boy understand what his dream meant?' he asked, passing Brother Renard his cup.

Brother Renard smiled in appreciation, reminding Solon of the man he had first known: a grumpy yet generous monk with a quick intelligence. But his hands shook as he took the cup, and he seemed more frail than ever. He took a long draught before continuing.

'The dream invaded the boy's sleep more than once. He told his father about it. He hoped his father would understand what it meant, because what occurs when a person is asleep means as much as what happens when he is awake.'

The world Solon lived in believed that ideas came in dreams, or were sent by witches or wizards, angels or demons, even gods or monsters. The origin of any idea or dream was important, making ideas either especially dangerous or incredibly brilliant. As he learned more about the world, Solon had begun to wonder: who decided which ideas were good and which were bad? Which held truths and which lies?

'But although the boy's father was a clever man, he was a poor, uneducated miller, and his son's dream terrified him,' Brother Renard continued, gulping the last of his perry. 'At first, he ignored his son's restless nights. But word began to spread that the miller's son was having visions. The lack of sleep was making the boy weak. He was no longer any help to his father in the mill.'

'Then what happened?'

'Then it rained for weeks,' said the old monk, exhaustion hunching his shoulders and weakening his voice. 'The turnips, leeks and cabbages rotted in the fields. The villagers started to get hungry, and when a wolf carried off the village's last healthy goat, anger set in like the chill in winter.'

'They blamed the boy and his dreams,' said Solon.

'Of course they did. And they gathered at the well, deciding that something had to be done about the boy. The angry villagers marched on the miller's cottage, wielding pickaxes and fiery torches, leaving the miller with no choice. He exiled his only son to the wilds of the Scottish forest.

'The boy journeyed across the Highlands until one day he stopped to fill his water pouch at a rocky shore. There in front of him was the recognizable outline of an island. The island of the silver-winged stag. He was able to fend for himself there, for the island was rich in fruits and the soil moist and fertile. Over time, the boy became a man. And when he did, he built a fortress, establishing the monastery on the island of Auchinmurn: a safe haven for those who dream and the things they dream about.'

Solon gaped. This was the story of the first monk of the Order of Era Mina.

The old monk paused, staring distractedly at the fire blazing in the hearth.

'What happened to the white peryton in the boy's dream?' asked Solon at last.

The old monk leaned towards the boy. The fire spat and crackled between them.

'It returned to its island and looked across the divide. It watched in grief as what remained of its twin's shadow crawled into a hollow in the earth at the centre of the smaller island . . . and disappeared.'

Outside Brother Renard's tiny cell, Solon heard the screech of gulls. He thought of the winged stag's mournful cries. His peryton.

'The white stag ached with loss,' the old monk whispered. 'So one night it flew high into the heavens above its twin's island, Era Mina, beating its silver wings so fast that it sounded like swarms of bees.

'And across the water in a thatched hut, the sleeping boy heard it call to him in his dream.'

TWENTY-SIX

There was a loud rustling in the trees outside the old monk's window. A snapping of branches, then mumbled voices and running footsteps.

'Someone's been listening to us!' exclaimed the old monk. His panic played like the tight strings of a lute in Solon's head. 'See who is lurking out there. This story is not for everyone's ears. Even among my brothers, there is a small number who would do their worst to get their hands on this manuscript. Especially before it is completed.'

'Why do they want it before it's completed?' asked Solon, confused.

'This book and Era Mina hold the keys to everything I've been telling you!' Brother Renard's voice rose an octave with agitation. 'Haven't you heard anything I've been saying, my boy? The darkness! The black peryton's shadow! It is seeping towards us!'

Solon unlocked the shutters and flung them open. A rush of sea air whooshed into the room as he squinted against the late afternoon sun, searching for the eavesdroppers, looking first in the trees beneath the window and then farther in the distance to the water's edge.

He thought he saw two hooded figures hurrying away.

He dropped down from the stone sill and pulled out the key hanging around his neck on a ribbon of leather. 'I must go,' he said as he prepared to unlock the door. 'But I'll return soon.'

'But the rest of what I must tell you cannot wait,' said the old monk fretfully. 'I may not have much time left.'

'What I have to do cannot wait either. I'll return as soon as I can.'

Solon pulled the heavy door shut and turned the key, dropping it back underneath his tunic. He leaped down the stairs, careening clumsily off the walls in his rush to get outside and down to the cove after the disappearing figures. At the door, he unlatched the hook and charged out into the fading daylight and the thick canopy of the forest.

He made his way quickly to the water, dodging round brothers working in the fields and gardens. The monastery's numbers had held steady at thirteen for as long as Solon could remember. Most of the work of the farm that surrounded the monastery was done by the monks themselves, with help from one or two men and women from the villages. The two monks tilling the kitchen gardens stared curiously after him, and a brother drawing on a bench near the Abbey's stables greeted Solon with a wave as he sprinted past.

At the water's edge, Solon hopscotched along the rocky shore, but he had lost them. Disappointment flooded through him. He slumped on the moss-covered rocks.

'Lost your best friend?'

Solon whipped round in surprise. The stranger was tall and thin with shiny black hair swept off his face, a jagged scar running through a trimmed dark beard and blue-grey eyes that gave his face a generous expression. His robes were cinched tightly round his waist as if he was wearing someone else's habit, an odd-looking striped scarf looped around his neck.

He reminded Solon of someone, but the young man could not put his mind to it. Perhaps he had seen him in the monastery. Solon knew all the monks personally, but he was ashamed to admit that he had been neglectful of the other men who kept the day-to-day tasks of the monastery and its lands running smoothly while the monks were copying, illustrating and binding books: labours of love that could take as long as a year at a time.

'I trust you won't give me away?' the stranger asked. His accent was that of a native Scot, but one who had learned to soften the guttural sounds of his consonants. His enunciations had a similar rhythm and pitch to the Abbot, who had travelled to places across the oceans. 'I come here when I can, and paint all over the island.'

'No, sir. Secrets are fully safe with me,' replied Solon.

The man had clearly been washing paintbrushes in one of the tidal pools. Solon stared curiously at his pots of inks lined up neatly in compartments inside a wooden basket with a long leather strap. He lifted out one of the pots. It was shaped like a mug, but Solon could see its contents clearly.

He held the vessel up to the man and tapped it. 'What is this?'

'It's called . . . glass,' replied the man.

He seemed uneasy. Solon strained to read his fears the way the Abbot was able to do with the old monk, but picked up nothing . . . except a prickly drift of disquiet.

Setting the vessel back inside the basket, Solon

95

ran his fingers quickly across the lining of the case: a light, soft fabric. The basket and its insides were nothing like the ones his mother and his sisters made from rushes and seaweeds, which always smelled of herring no matter how many herbs they soaked the weeds in. This basket smelled of flowers and fresh air.

'What are you doing down here?' asked Solon.

'Ach, lad, I've been capturing the monastery and the islands on my paper— I mean, parchment. I paint landscapes.'

'Landscapes?' Solon understood the meaning of the word, but it was base and vulgar as subject matter for art. Why waste your gift on a scene that was visible to the eye every day?

He looked at the man's work perched on the easel. Unable to restrain himself, Solon let out a long whistle.

The stranger had captured the monastery in the fading daylight in thick strokes of colour like nothing Solon had ever seen before. The rows of spindly fir trees were no more than tall strips of differing shades of green inks, the rocky cliff a patch of grey, the water bright splashes of blue with spots of white dabbed upon it, the part-built tower outlined in black, and the sun a pink line on the horizon; but when taken together, when seen in their entirety, the inks blended, and the painting looked like the man had held a mirror up to the scene in front of him.

'It is beautiful,' said Solon in wonder. 'It is as if the light reflecting on the water has been transposed to your parchment.'

He looked into the man's eyes, then back at the luminosity of the painting. 'Are you a member of the Order of Era Mina?'

The man cocked his head. 'Era Mina?'

'It is the name for the Order of monks who live here. Many of them are Animare. They . . . we have faculties to . . . to enliven our art, to add to its brilliance.'

'Era Mina . . . *Animare*! Of course!' The man laughed, a deep throaty guffaw.

Solon took a step away from the stranger, his flesh suddenly chilled. 'Who are you?'

Before the man could answer, Solon lost his footing on the damp moss, fell backwards and cracked his head on the rocks.

After checking that the boy was still breathing, the stranger made sure Solon was as comfortable as possible. He stared down sympathetically.

'I do hate to leave you like this, my young friend, but time is of the essence,' he said.

TWENTY-SEVEN

The Abbey
Present Day

When Matt was younger, he'd often sneaked out of bed early on Saturday mornings before Em woke so he could have some time alone in the flat with his mum. After a while, he felt that Saturday mornings belonged only to him and her—until his mum had been blackmailed into working for an international art-forgery ring, and their Saturday mornings together were abruptly brought to an end because she had to paint.

After that, Matt stopped rising early on Saturday mornings.

Now everything had changed again. No matter what everyone at the Abbey was doing together to find Sandie, Saturday mornings were Matt's time to investigate what had happened to his mum—on his own.

Jeannie was in the kitchen making scones when Matt came downstairs. Without saying a word, she handed him a glass of milk and a plate with one of Matt's favourite handheld breakfasts on it—two flaky wheat biscuits with chocolate spread slathered between them. Weeks ago, he and Zach had come up with the idea of creating breakfasts that you held in one hand while you played video games with the other.

'Mind ye don't leave a trail of crumbs in all the books,' Jeannie warned, as Matt headed off, plate and glass in hand. 'Or I'll be hearing from Mr R.'

Inside the huge library, Matt set his plate on a table next to a cabinet with glass doors and shelves packed with over-sized leather-bound books. The cabinet held mostly old maps and prints that no one had looked at for years.

With its smell of old books and lemon polish, this room was one of Matt's favourites. It fed his obsession with old maps of the islands and ancient drawings of the Abbey, and held a wealth of both—thanks to the fact that all of the Calders in the past had been avid book collectors. Some of the drawings and maps that he'd recently been checking out were still spread across a table in the middle of the room. The walls were covered with books and, where there wasn't a shelf, art. Carvings of local birds covered the great wooden doors. Sometimes when Matt caught his grandfather deep in thought or lost in one of the library books, the bulbous puffin in the middle bobbed its head knowingly.

Busts of all the Calder ancestors who had lived on the island and owned the Abbey were carved in white stone and set into a series of small niches evenly spaced along the high stepped ceiling. Em thought it a little creepy that their ancestors were always watching them from above, but Matt found them comforting. His favourite was the guy with a scar down his cheek. He always saluted him when he entered the room.

Matt unlocked the glass cabinet, sliding the door open as far as he could. Then he shifted the biggest of the map books on to the floor under the table. As he lifted out a ragged folder of prints, the corner of the folder caught the edge of his plate. As if in slow motion, the plate and glass of milk began to topple off the end of the table towards the precious stack of maps underneath.

Matt flung the folder away from him like a Frisbee. He lunged at his falling breakfast, catching the glass in time and just saving the maps from a soaking. But he was too late for the plate, which clattered to the wood floor.

While he was on his knees brushing crumbs on to a folded sheet of sketch paper, a burst of colour caught his eye. It was from one of the prints that had fallen from the folder when he'd tossed it.

Balling up the paper, Matt dunked it into the bin across the room. He flipped through the prints as he returned them to the folder, searching for the one that had caught his eye. Most of them were impressions from medieval woodcuts, images of the monastery when it was founded. One showed the Abbey's ancient catacombs, and there were a number of etchings of the face of Jesus, the Virgin Mary, a few sheep and lots of haloed angels. He dismissed all but the sketch of the catacombs, which he rolled up and slid into his pocket, and an original painting of the Abbey.

This painting was quite unlike the others. Taking it over to the light table, Matt set it on the white, translucent surface and turned on the light. Looking at the picture in this way meant he could see the details of the artist's strokes and—the part that always made Matt's pulse quicken—anything that had been sketched or painted underneath.

There was nothing underneath this one. It was an Impressionist scene, and reminded Matt of

William Turner's paintings of the Thames and its ships. This artist had titled it *Skinner's Bog*. Matt knew the spot: a putrid marsh beside a couple of standing stones high up on Auchinmurn which were reputed to have mystical powers. The artist had painted from the edge of the bog, capturing the western façade of the Abbey in the distance, with the bay a band of blue-grey between the two islands and the rising sun a pink line on the horizon.

Matt took a magnifying glass from the light-table drawer and examined the watercolour brush strokes more closely. They had been applied quickly in the classic Impressionist style, and there were places where the colours had bled into each other more roughly than in other parts of the painting. The picture itself was the shape of a sheet of notebook paper. A whiff of rotting fish seeped out of it, a mixture of seaweed and Jeannie's pickled-herring sandwiches.

The smell shifted an idea in Matt's head, and he spotted what was wrong with the image. The tower on Era Mina wasn't there.

He knew from his research that the tower had been completed in 1263, and as such it was one of the oldest standing Celtic structures in the whole of Great Britain.

The Impressionists produced their new style of painting in the mid-nineteenth century. So how had an Impressionist captured the Abbey and the islands as they had been before 1263? There would have been no photographs to copy. All Matt had found in his research was a series of woodcuts depicting the history of the monastery. There had been no woodcut of the buildings.

A shot of adrenalin spiked Matt's pulse.

What if he and Em were not the only Animare whose powers were strong enough to time-travel through art?

The picture was most definitely worth hanging on to.

TWENTY-EIGHT

A crusading knight on a black stallion, a Templar cape with its signature red cross rising and falling behind him, was riding straight for Em as she ran for her life, trying desperately to escape his reach, breathlessly sprinting through a labyrinth of hedgerows and tangled paths. But no matter which direction she turned, the knight was always in front of her, always charging at her through a smoky white veil, the black horse's eyes fiery points of red.

Em woke up in a fright. Gasping for breath, she recognized after a moment of terror that she was not being chased, but was in her room at the Abbey, safe in her bed.

Grabbing the book fanned out on her pillow, she chucked it on to the floor.

'Stupid *Ivanhoe*.'

Simon banged on her bedroom door. 'The dock in thirty minutes,' he called. 'You three are on beach clean-up for your dangerous stunt last night.'

'Why so early?' mumbled Em.

'It's not early. So if you want breakfast before you get to work, you'd better hurry. Jeannie's not going to wait for much longer.'

Em staggered towards her bathroom, surprised that the clock was already showing 10 am. She got dressed slowly and headed for the stairs. The still-life with the modern goblet had been taken off the stair wall.

'Where's the painting?' she called down to Simon.

'Your grandpa has it,' Simon said, looking up at her from the foyer. 'We'll discuss that painting and your time-hopping after you've cleaned up the beach. There was a storm last night, so there should be lots for you to do.'

'Ugh!' said Em.

*   *   *

Over a late second breakfast of sliced bananas on toast, Matt explained what he'd discovered in the library, spreading the picture out across the table in front of the others.

'Maybe this artist's a time-traveller too,' he said, tapping the painting. 'An Impressionist painting of a medieval scene that no one's seen since the 1260s? It's obvious!'

'Oh man, it smells like something's died on that,' signed Zach, cupping his hand over his mouth.

'Gross,' said Em, pushing the last corner of her toast away.

'The beach won't clean itself,' Simon called from the garden. 'Let's go!'

Matt shoved the canvas under a table placemat and grabbed his coat. 'It'll be okay until we get back,' he told the others. 'You know Jeannie will stop for 'a wee blether' with her friends in Seaport. We'll be finished on the beach before she comes home. Last one to the water's edge does tonight's dishes.'

When they were bundled up against the autumn chill and the wind from the Atlantic, they raced each other across the sloping lawn to meet Simon on the dock. Matt won easily, but Em thought it was only because Zach was in pain from the thrashing.

At the end of the jetty, Simon passed a bin bag and a pair of rubber gloves to each of them, sending them off along the beach to pick up tourist rubbish and storm debris that had washed ashore the night before.

'Can you imagine how long it would take to clean up the banks of the Thames in 1871?' asked Matt, as they stuffed bags with beach rubbish.

'Would you please let that go for a while?' said Em. 'I'd like to not always be in trouble with the adults in our lives.' She glanced at Zach. 'How's your back?'

Zach was walking stiffly, not picking up much rubbish.

'It hurts,' he signed wryly. 'Skin feels tight when I bend. Some of the cuts are itching, too.'

'Next time,' said Matt, 'let's go somewhere that children get some respect.'

'Good luck finding that place,' signed Zach.

'Next time?' said Em, glowering at her brother as she dropped a soggy disposable nappy into her bag. 'Unless you want to keep doing disgusting chores like this every morning, I suggest we do not have a next time for a very long time.'

Zach and Matt glanced at each other. Em raised her hands to make them stop.

'I mean it! We're lucky that we made it back from that painting alive. If we keep breaking Animare rules like that, the Council of Guardians will come after us and bind us the second we turn sixteen for sure. Never mind what will happen if the stupid Hollow Earth Society find out about our newest talent.'

At moments like this Em wished her mother were here. She walked down to the water's edge and kicked at the waves angrily.

Where are you, Mum? I miss you so much.

Matt came down the beach to join her. Putting his hand on her shoulder, he said, 'Mum's okay, Em. I think we'd feel it if she wasn't.'

'I just wish we knew where she was,' said Em mournfully.

Zach sloshed around in a tidal pool next to them, digging up rocks and examining them for fossils. Above the shore, the traffic on the island's only main road to Seaport was sparse, the school summer holidays over and tourist season dwindling to a dozen or so visitors with every ferry trip from Largs. Em looked beseechingly at her brother.

'Let's agree to no more time travel, Matt,' she pleaded. 'It scared me. I didn't like being . . . being so far from home.'

She realized that, for the first time, she really felt like the Abbey and the island had become her home.

'Besides, we need to put our energies into finding Mum, not into developing new ways to worry Grandpa, Simon or Jeannie. Agreed?'

'No,' said Matt. 'Not agreed at all.'

'Please, Matt,' Em pleaded, her anxiety churning up the water in Zach's tidal pool. Several unnaturally high waves in the bay started rolling into the shore. Combing his hair off his face, Matt held Em's gaze, trying to practise what he'd learned from Simon about drawing out Em's fears before they settled inside her imagination. That was never good for Em, and often bad for all of them.

106

Particularly when Em's fears animated themselves and became a danger to others.

'We're going to find Mum, especially now that Grandpa is home and able to help us,' said Matt firmly, 'but think about it. If Simon's right after all, and we're the only Animare who have ever time-travelled using a painting, then there can't be a rule about no time travel. So, technically, we haven't broken any rules.'

'He's got a point, Em,' signed Zach, high-fiving Matt's logic.

'No, he hasn't!' shouted Em.

She tossed her full rubbish bag over her shoulder and ran up the beach. Behind her, a huge wave crashed into the boys, drenching both of them.

Watching from the wooden bench at the end of the Abbey's jetty, Simon rubbed his temples, feeling the tension. It was probably a result of the growing pains of three newly minted teenagers, nothing more.

TWENTY-NINE

After a late lunch of soup and sandwiches, Renard called the children and Simon to the library. Em was still smarting at the fact that the boys had ganged up on her earlier, but the boys didn't seem to notice.

As they entered the room, Matt saluted the scarred bust in its niche.

'Why do you always salute that statue?' asked Zach, catching Matt's gesture.

Matt shrugged. 'The dude looks fierce with that scar down his cheek. I'd have liked to have met him. Apparently, he's the one who salvaged the Abbey from its medieval ruins and rebuilt it the way it is now.'

Zach looked at the bust. 'What's his name?'

Matt shrugged. 'Don't know.' Simon had never said.

At one of the tables in front of the windows, Renard had set out the items Sandie had left behind the night she disappeared: the rusty old key and the page from *The Book of Beasts*. He'd hung the still-life with Jeannie's pewter goblet on the wall directly above it.

When Zach and the twins were settled in front of him with Simon leaning against the French doors out to the garden, Renard began to speak.

'After some careful thought on the still-life, and after talking with Simon about the recent evolution

108

of your abilities, I've come to a decision.'

Matt and Em looked nervously at each other.

Do you think he's going to send us away?

Don't be ridiculous.

My dad wouldn't let him send you away, Zach added in answer to Em's question. *And neither would I.*

'I've decided,' continued Renard, 'that if you are ever to understand how truly important and unique your hybrid talents are, you must learn to use your powers wisely. And to do that, I need you to understand the history of our kind.'

Jeannie pushed open the library's double doors with her foot, carrying a tray with a pot of coffee, three glasses of chocolate milk and slices of pound cake slathered in jam. When the cake had been devoured, Matt and Zach wiped their milk moustaches on their sleeves.

'Barbarians,' Simon laughed, looking at the boys with disapproval.

'Grandpa, Simon's taught us a lot about our history already,' said Em, patting her mouth with her napkin. 'We know that Calders have always lived on the islands since before even the Vikings, and that the monks of Era Mina were the first to bring together Animare and Guardians for protection.'

Renard nodded. 'Good. But I'd like to go back even further. Because, given what you demonstrated yesterday, the speed and emphasis of these lessons must be increased. You have to learn about the islands' geology and your unique connection to it. And all the information you need can be found in Duncan Fox's diary.'

'Duncan Fox is the artist who painted *The*

109

Demon Within!' Em gasped. Memories of the horrible painting still haunted her. The red, skinless monster . . . 'The painting Mum copied. The picture Dad's bound in, down in the Abbey vault.'

'Ow!' Matt cried, as Charles Dickens's *Hard Times* suddenly soared off its shelf and smacked him on the back of the head.

'Em,' said Renard gently, as the entire shelf of Romantic poets started to shiver. 'You have nothing to fear while you are here in the Abbey with us.'

Zach reached under the table and squeezed Em's hand, calming her fears which were making the books shake.

As the books settled, Renard pointed at the bust of the scarred man, high up in its niche. 'That's Duncan Fox, up there.'

'Him?' Matt said in shock. 'The dude with the scar? And he's the one who painted . . .' Matt couldn't bring himself to say it. 'You mean, he's *family*?'

'His wife was a Calder like us,' said Renard. 'Duncan Fox owned these islands and the ruins of the Abbey in the mid-nineteenth century, and although he spent most of his early life in London while the Abbey was being rebuilt, this was later to become his beloved home.'

THIRTY

'Duncan Fox was the artist who started the original Hollow Earth Society, wasn't he?' asked Em. 'The Society that swore to keep Hollow Earth and all its monsters a secret from the world?'

'Yes,' replied Renard. 'Fox started the original Hollow Earth Society because, according to his diary, he once glimpsed Hollow Earth for himself. What he saw there was so terrifying that he wanted to bury the knowledge of its existence for ever. Reduce it to a myth, and ultimately let it be forgotten altogether. Most importantly, he wanted to protect it from any Animare powerful enough to use the mystical tools needed to open Hollow Earth again.'

In her head, Em was already imagining what these mystical tools might be. As she dwelt on this exciting question, a black hole opened in the air above the table, and an avalanche of sparkling silver wands, a gilded mirror and a shiny, gold sceptre, crusted with green gems, fell at her feet.

The room was silent until the treasures and trinkets stopped piling up. Simon and Renard looked at each other and burst out laughing.

'Sorry,' Em said hastily, throwing herself over the animations, exploding them in a confetti burst of light.

Em, get a grip. You're not a kid any more.

I said *sorry!*

'Hollow Earth is at the centre of the island of Era Mina,' Renard continued. 'The only way to reach it is through the images on the walls in the island's caves. But you cannot do that without using the sacred bone quill, a pen made from the antlers of the black peryton, to animate *The Book of Beasts*. Had the monks been able to finish the book, they would have closed the portal to Hollow Earth entirely, but they didn't . . . they couldn't. And now no one knows what happened to the rest of the book, or to the bone quill.'

'There's a *black* peryton?' said Em.

'These islands are a safe haven for Animare and their Guardians because of the islands' special properties,' answered Renard. 'You see, before Hollow Earth became a place to trap and bind the terrible monsters from the world of our myths, it was the place that created two of the most powerful of those beasts: the white peryton and its twin, the black.'

'Two islands, two perytons and two of us,' said Matt apprehensively. The weight of all this information was settling uncomfortably in his head.

'There is an interesting parallel here, yes,' Renard agreed.

'Did Dad know all of this, about the island and its powers and Hollow Earth?' Matt's heart was beating fast, his head still smarting from the book. 'Did you tell him about it?'

'When he turned sixteen, it was Malcolm's time to learn,' replied Renard. 'Since ancient times, a Calder has lived on the island in order to protect Hollow Earth and keep it—and the powers of the island—a secret from the world. But Malcolm chose a different path. The path of power, greed

112

and ambition. Your father is lost to us, Matt, because of the choices he made. I'm sorry.'

Without warning, a paperweight bust of the Scottish poet Robert Burns on Renard's desk began babbling out one of his poems, his eyes bulging from his marble head, his short pony-tail flapping up and down in the air.

Em looked white. Zach grabbed her hand again.

It's going to be okay.

I feel sick. My tummy hurts.

'The monks of Era Mina understood the world was changing,' said Renard. 'Science and learning were replacing magic and superstition, and they believed that such progress should be welcomed. They made it their mission to use the unique powers of the island and the abilities of their Animare brothers to trap the beasts from the dangerous, magical past by drawing them—*binding* them—into Hollow Earth using *The Book of Beasts*. But it remained unfinished, and the job half done. Hollow Earth remains a danger to anyone prepared to use the bone quill to unbind the beasts within.'

'The monks of Era Mina sound kind of like Noah and his ark,' Zach signed. 'Gathering up all the beasts and monsters of the old world.'

Renard tapped the frame of the still-life on the wall. 'I thought about this painting most of last night. I believe it is connected with Sandie's disappearance, while Sandie's disappearance is tied up with the history of this island and Malcolm's quest to find and open Hollow Earth.'

'You think Mum painted the goblet into the painting,' Matt said with excitement. 'Don't you?'

'I do,' said Renard. 'It was a clever choice of

113

object. Something that only we would notice.'

'She wanted to tell us where she's gone!' Matt burst out.

Em jumped up. 'We've always wondered why she left without telling us anything.'

'Exactly!' said Matt. He picked up the mysterious old key from the table and rolled it between his fingers. He felt as if they were getting closer to unravelling the mysteries that Sandie had left behind. 'She grabs one of the goblets from the kitchen and animates it into this still-life. Then she returns the painting to the wall, here where we'd notice it.'

Em fetched the magnifying glass to study the painting more closely. Filled with impatient energy, Matt grabbed the magnifying glass from his sister and shoved her aside. The key in his hand clattered to the floor.

'Cut it out, both of you,' said Simon sharply.

Zach crawled under the table and retrieved the key. But when he stood up, instead of putting the key back in its place, he held it up in front of the desk in the painting. Directly in front of the keyhole on the desk drawer.

THIRTY-ONE

'No way you're animating into another painting,' said Simon firmly, as everyone stared at the still-life on the library wall.

'But Mum may have left us a message in that desk,' Matt said.

'I don't care,' said Simon. He had taken the key from Zach. 'Until we've exhausted every possibility for what this key might mean in our reality right here,' he thumped his hand on the table for emphasis, 'I forbid you to go to another one.'

Matt could feel rage rising in his gut. Em glared at him.

Calm down. You're not helping our chances.

He can't forbid us, Em! He's not our father and he's not my Guardian!

If you keep losing your temper, he'll inspirit you. And then we'll never be able to do anything without his encouragement, so please cool it.

Matt was about to open his mouth again, when Renard suddenly spoke.

'Sit. Both of you. Please.'

The twins sat.

'As difficult as it is for you to understand all that's happened here since your arrival, you must know that we only have your best interests at heart.'

Matt hated it when adults said this to him. His mum had said it the day they had fled London, and

115

now look what had happened.

Renard went on. 'I agree with Simon. We should be absolutely sure that we have a reason to animate, especially into this particular painting.'

'Why?' asked Matt, doing his best to temper his tone.

'If we assume that this painting is by Duncan Fox—and everything would indicate this to be true: style, date etc—then the date on the picture troubles me,' said Renard. 'If 1848 is correct, then it was the last painting Fox completed before he discovered Hollow Earth, and made it his mission to do what he could to keep it sealed and protected. 1848 is the last time that Hollow Earth was in danger of being opened.'

The twins digested this.

'*If* Duncan Fox painted it,' Renard repeated. He smiled slightly, as if enjoying a private joke. Then he opened his desk drawer and took out a red clothbound journal.

'Is that Fox's diary?' asked Matt.

Renard nodded. He passed the journal to Em. Matt and Zach gazed over her shoulder as she flipped through the yellowed musty pages. It was filled with words and sketches.

'I've never seen that before,' said Simon.

'The diary was found shortly before we bound Malcolm,' Renard said. 'I haven't shared it around much since then.'

'Go back,' said Matt, directing Em to a page with some of Fox's drawings and pointing at the biggest one. 'Isn't that the Abbey?'

That's like the picture I found this morning, Em. But this one has the tower under construction.

Maybe the painting you found was just unfinished.

116

No, I think one was painted after the other. I think Duncan Fox is my time-traveller. Now I really *want to meet the dude.*

'It certainly looks like the Abbey,' said Em, doing her best to ignore Matt's voice in her head. Zach tilted his head for a better view and nodded his agreement.

'The diary tells us a great deal,' said Renard. He looked at the still-life. 'But it makes no mention of this painting. Which strikes me as curious. I don't think this still-life was painted by Duncan Fox at all.'

Matt frowned. 'Then who?'

'I think it may have been painted by your mother.'

THIRTY-TWO

Everyone began throwing questions at Renard, even Simon. The din in the room was so loud that Jeannie rushed in to see what the ruckus was about.

'Em,' said Simon, 'you look pale. Are you feeling okay?'

'Just a tummy ache,' Em whispered. 'But don't tell Jeannie. She'll make me drink a cabbage-water tonic.'

Zach picked up the key and held it up in front of the desk drawer on the still-life again. 'Now there's even more reason to believe this might fit that lock,' he signed.

'Em and I *need* to animate into that painting,' said Matt at once.

'They may be on to something, Renard,' Simon murmured.

'But where might they end up?' Renard gestured at the painting. 'If that picture is by Fox, you will end up in 1848. If it was painted by your mother, you may find that you only travel back two months. You travel to the time in which the image was created, do you not?'

The question made Em feel light-headed. Outside it was drizzling. The light and the rain reflecting on the great mirror installation made the trees look as if they were walking backwards on the lawn.

'It's too risky. I won't allow it,' said Renard

decisively.

'What if I went with them into the painting?' Simon suggested. 'We know they're strong enough to shift me, too. Then at least I'm there, wherever we end up.'

Em felt Zach's anger buffet her like a fan blowing against her body.

We wouldn't be gone long, Zach.

I don't have to like being left behind.

Grandpa's not coming with us either.

He's an old man.

Zach!

'We open the drawer with the key,' continued Simon, 'find what Sandie has left for us—assuming the key works—and come directly back.'

'Sounds like a plan,' said Matt confidently.

If Grandpa doesn't let us go now, Em, we'll go on our own later.

Matt! We wouldn't do that.

I would.

Em stared at her brother. *You don't really mean that.*

Matt shrugged off her dismay. At long last he had a clue to his mum's disappearance, and he was not letting it go.

Simon loudly cleared his throat. The twins noticed the room had quietened.

'What were you two squabbling about in your heads?' asked Renard.

Matt stole a glance at Em. 'We think we can control our animation so that we don't time-travel,' he said.

Zach could feel Em's anxiety tightening the muscles in his neck.

Are you okay?

119

Em nodded at Zach, but she wasn't okay at all. She hated it when Matt lied, and she hated it that she was glad that he had.

'Fine,' said Renard reluctantly. 'But Simon goes with you and you animate into the painting directly. Retrieve whatever clue Sandie has left and then animate back . . . immediately. Understood?'

*   *   *

Simon stood between the twins with his fingers hooked on the waistbands of their jeans, leaving their hands free to animate. Renard had moved the still-life from the wall to an easel in the centre of the library, around which they were all gathered.

In unison, the twins locked the image of the painting in their imaginations and closed their eyes. Matt leaned in front of Simon and began drawing the desk first. While he captured that, Em tackled the specific objects sitting on the desk, starting with the skull. She loved drawing skulls.

Wait!

Em's eyes popped open a beat before she heard Zach's whistle. Matt lifted his hand from the page, the paper already shimmering with lines of light. Zach grabbed the key they'd almost forgotten and slipped it quickly into his dad's pocket.

The twins resumed their drawing, fingers flying, becoming more translucent with every stroke. Soon the three of them were made up of light and colour. With a whoosh, they shot into the centre of the still-life, sending tiny haloes of light into the air above it.

'As long as we can see the particles of light,' Renard murmured, 'they're all okay.'

120

THIRTY-THREE

The Middle Ages
The Monastery of Era Mina

Solon sat up with a bump the size of an egg on the back of his head. He sensed the peryton's presence before he felt its touch. The wind had shifted direction and become a warm breeze. The force of the receding tide drained the water from the pool where Solon was submerged, flipping him on to his stomach.

Coughing and gagging, drenched and shivering, Solon expelled a bucket's worth of slimy, salt water. At the sharp insistent prod of the peryton's gleaming antler, he sat up. His head ached. Leaning back on his elbows, he looked around the darkening cove for the stranger and his painting. Where had he gone?

Satisfied that Solon was okay, the peryton leaped on to the rocks in front of the cove and took flight, disappearing like a spray of stars in the darkening sky. Solon watched it go with groggy eyes.

After Vespers in the Abbey, Solon headed for the refectory with the other brothers for his evening meal. Overhead, heavy clouds scudded across the sky. Brother Thomas, the monastery's master baker and passable cook, lamented as he served Solon his meal that a bad storm was coming in from the lands to the north.

'Ach, I can feel it in here,' he said, rubbing beneath the knee of his weakened left leg.

Brother Thomas's leg injury was the consequence of once wrestling a boar on to a spit for a royal feast. The weakness in his leg had done little to impair his movements. With or without the aid of a crutch, he was fast on his feet.

Brother Thomas had a number of body parts that talked to him on occasions of astrological and agrarian significance. His nose smelled a full moon rising, his ears heard the turnips growing. Solon's favourite was generally Brother Thomas's eye.

Brother Thomas had lost an eye at the point of a Viking sword when he was a boy. A leather eye patch created by the Abbey's tanner covered the socket. On the evening of the winter solstice, Brother Thomas would lead his fellow monks to the water's edge where he'd lift his patch, turn the cross-stitched hole towards the setting sun and predict the severity of the remaining cold season.

'The eye sees ice forming on the horizon,' he'd claim with great import before leading the procession back to the great hall for mulled wine.

Solon was never entirely sure if Brother Thomas's gift was another special quality of the monks of Era Mina, or simply one monk's unique way of making sense of the world.

He took his meal outside to the rocks below the kitchens, willing to tolerate the chill of the night in order to think about all that had happened that day: the eavesdroppers, and the oddly familiar stranger; Brother Renard's story of the twin stags, and the crack on his head.

It was too much to make sense of without counsel. Not for the first time, Solon wished that

122

his beloved master were not so hampered with his own trials. Digging into the remains of his rabbit stew, he found the last morsel of meat before licking the bowl clean.

His head still thumping, he climbed back up to the kitchens: two square brick buildings close to the water and away from the main monastery. Keeping the buildings separate ensured that any stray fires would be doused before they reached the monastery. At the top of the rocks, Solon felt the first drop of rain.

In matters of the heavenly bodies and his own, Brother Thomas was rarely wrong.

THIRTY-FOUR

When the storm hit the islands, it brought winds that bent the tallest trees and rains that lashed down in grey sheets, pushing the sea to the heels of the monastery. That night, the islands were not a safe place for man or beast. The drenched monks settled the horses in the stables, locking the doors and barring the shutters moments before thunder hammered the sky and arrows of light shot across the darkness.

Watching the storm from the door of the kitchens, Solon remembered Brother Renard. The young man had promised to return, but the blow to his head had made him forget. He had to get back to his old master's cell right away, but with the water rising so quickly in the courtyard, finding another path around the monastery was prudent.

He briefly contemplated drawing a way through the ferocious storm. Then he heard Brother Renard's voice in his head, speaking words from long ago.

'The powers of a monk of Era Mina must be used for the glory of God and the benefit of mankind, and never for selfish gain.'

Trying to avoid getting drenched or drowned were not worthy reasons to indulge his fledgling abilities.

The sealed, waterproof catacombs were the only way. Solon shivered. The labyrinth of tunnels snaking under the monastery and its outbuildings held the martyrs of the Order, monks murdered during the early days of the monastery when the surrounding land was a haven for Saxon raiders and Pictish barbarians. Venturing into the catacombs meant passing the chamber of crypts, and passing the chamber of crypts meant passing the mummified bodies of those monks watching over the martyrs as they made their way to Paradise.

The nearest entrance to the catacombs was in the cellar under the kitchen. Solon pushed through the kitchen doors and down the cobbled steps to the cellar. He had to roll away two full wine barrels to get to the small oak door that was his entrance to the tunnels.

He lifted an unlit torch from its bracket on the wall, dipped it in the bucket of sheep's fat kept for this purpose and struck a flint. The flame filled the room with long shadows. Solon shoved open the door and, holding the torch high above his head, climbed down the steep, narrow steps into the catacombs.

A rough layer of sand whispered beneath his feet. It had seeped into the tunnels from past storms and regular blustery island winds. At the first tunnel, Solon stopped and rolled the collar of his tunic up under his chin. He started forward in the direction of the north tower, where Brother Renard's room was located. Rats scuttled over his feet the deeper into the maze he went, colonies of bats whipping overhead when they swarmed from their nests high in the alcoves. His torch was disturbing their peace.

As he went on, the tunnels became lower and

125

narrower, forcing Solon to hunch over as he walked. The violence of the storm above ground was barely audible down here.

After a few yards, the stench in the catacombs was so overwhelming it forced Solon to breath through his mouth. The smell got worse the closer he came to the chamber of the crypts. The stink of the thick clay, sand, sulphur and cod liver oil that the monks slathered over bodies of the dead soon caked Solon's throat. And as if those smells were not awful enough, Solon could detect the cloying perfumes from the wilting petals in the monk's anointing oils, trying and failing to mask the stench.

He had to stop for a moment to catch his breath. When he did, he gagged, swallowed bile and began to cough noisily. Slapping his hand over his mouth, he was suddenly afraid his coughing would disturb the dead.

A mighty gust of fetid air suddenly knocked out his torch flame, followed by a loud crack up ahead in the crypt—as if someone had broken a branch, or snapped a twig.

Someone else was down here.

Solon backed up against the wall, admonishing himself for daring to come down to the catacombs alone. This was one of the most sacred places on the island—and also the scariest.

He heard angry hisses, a mumbled yelp and then what sounded like footsteps. But not ordinary footsteps. Footsteps that sounded as if someone was dragging a heavy weight behind them.

Could the dead walk?

Pressing his back to the wall, Solon set down the useless torch and eased away from the chamber, the stone scratching through the cloth of his tunic.

126

The noises appeared to be following him. By the time Solon realized that he had come too far, it was too late. He had backed into a dead end.

With no other choice, Solon retraced his steps towards the chamber, keeping his hands flat on the wall to guide him. But the dragging footsteps and the muffled voices had shifted. Now they sounded to Solon as if they were *behind* him. That was impossible. Behind him was a dead end.

The air felt as if it was being sucked from the catacombs. Had someone opened a door along one of the other tunnels?

Keeping his back to the damp, scratchy wall, Solon slipped into the crypt itself. He dropped behind one of the tombs and listened.

Snap. Snap. Snap.

His skin crawled as if a rat had dropped on to his shoulders and scampered down his back. The realization of what he was hearing struck him with full force. He fought back his horror.

Man or beast, something was breaking the bones of the mummified monks.

Using his finger as a quill, Solon sketched an image hastily on the sandy ground. As soon as he finished, he cowered behind the tomb, cupping his left hand in his right. At first, he didn't believe his faculties had served him at all. Then a tingling tickled his finger, a tiny spark shot out from his knuckle and a tiny flame burst to life on the edge of his nail. Solon wanted to cheer, but in the circumstances thought better of it.

Stretching himself across the ground while staying tight up against the tomb, Solon cupped his finger so that only a pale glow was visible. He peered out into the circular chamber.

Brother Cornelius was climbing up the wall towards one of the most ancient mummified monks, strapped into a niche in the ceiling of the crypt. The mummy's head was bowed against his chest, his skull hidden under a rich, hooded, purple cowl. Brother Thomas was doing the same thing on the other side of the chamber. They were both reaching up under the monks' habits and snapping their clasped hands apart as if searching for something.

'Cornelius,' said Brother Thomas suddenly. 'Where is that light coming from?'

Solon froze.

'The eternal torches must still have some glow about them, Thomas,' soothed Cornelius. 'That is all. Hurry. Our Prophet says time is our enemy. He must have the quill and *The Book of Beasts,* or we are all doomed. That Solon returned unscathed from Skinner's Bog and survived the Grendel has already complicated matters.'

Brother Cornelius dropped to the ground, dragging his damaged leg across the chamber. He then awkwardly climbed up to the niche where the third and last mummy was ensconced.

What prophet? Solon thought in confusion. *What quill?* Cornelius's and Thomas's macabre behaviour and furtive conversation were beginning to terrify him. Clearly, he wasn't meant to have returned from Skinner's Bog at all.

He had seen and heard enough to know that he was in grave danger. He wiped the image from the floor with his sleeve, the light extinguishing from his finger immediately. Crawling backwards out of the chamber, he stood up and sprinted back along the dark tunnels, towards the kitchen cellar and out into the storm.

THIRTY-FIVE

Duncan Fox's Studio
London
1848

Em landed face down on an oriental rug that smelled of cigars and wet dog, the nose of a confused beagle bumping up against her own. Matt landed on his feet, one on the rug and one inside a brass spittoon shaped like a turtle. Simon crashed head first into a potted palm tree.

The beagle leaped to its feet almost as quickly as Em, who in an instant knew they had animated beyond the painting and into the past again. It felt like a punch to the gut. She had wanted the painting to be by her mother, not Fox. Her disappointment made her ache.

Time-travelling to a Victorian artist's studio gave Em a queasy feeling. She had never seen a place with so much furniture. Every open space had chairs: wooden, cushioned, low-backed and one looking like a throne. Em squinted at the throne. The lid on the seat suggested it was an old toilet chair.

Every space that didn't have a chair had a side table, and every side table was cluttered with books and figurines. Then there were tall lamps and short lamps, all powered by gas, the tubing running along the rafters and out of sight. The entire place looked

129

like it was one spark away from a blaze.

The walls were covered in framed and unframed paintings. The front windows were made of stained glass with four heraldic shields across the top panes. One looked like the crest of the Abbey, with the peryton on it.

And then Em looked up, noting the roof made of glass, the rows of skylights open to the late afternoon sun, and knew exactly where they had landed.

She helped her brother lift his foot from the squishy muck in the spittoon, then yanked him to the middle of the over-furnished room, her disappointment at not seeing her mother drowned out by her sudden excitement. 'Matt! Do you realize where we are?'

Matt gawked. 'It's our flat!'

'What?' said Simon, setting the palm upright. Straightening up, he hit his head on a birdcage hanging from one of the rafters. The bird squawked angrily.

'Our old flat!' exclaimed Matt. 'When we lived in London.'

They suddenly spotted a man standing at the other side of the room next to an easel. His dark hair was slicked back behind his ears, a scar running through his short black beard, and in front of him was the desk they had come to open, topped with the skull, the candelabra, the mirrored glass and Jeannie's pewter goblet. He looked like a handsome head teacher with his hands folded behind his back and his posture ramrod straight.

'That was as grand a theatrical entrance as I've seen,' said the man. 'Worthy of the Adelphi Theatre.'

Wiping his paint-stained hands on a white cloth over his shoulder, he offered Simon his hand first. 'This may be rather a shock to you, sir, but I am Duncan Fox. This is September of 1848, the eleventh year of the reign of Victoria. Welcome to my London.'

'It's not as much of a shock as you might think,' said Simon, accepting Fox's hand and shaking it vigorously.

Matt was absorbing the details of the room where, more than a century in the future, he'd spend his childhood. It was just one massive room, the building a large Victorian mansion not yet divided up into flats. His smile at Fox was a little dazed.

'You must be Matt,' Fox said. Then he turned to Em, bowing slightly. 'And you must be Emily. I have heard a great deal about all of you.'

'How do you know who we are?' Em asked curiously.

'Because,' said a familiar voice from the hallway, 'I've been expecting you.'

Sandie was rushing up the stairs in a long, purple, velvet dress, arms outstretched.

'*Mum!*'

The twins flew into their mother's arms, knocking all three of them against the wall in a flood of sobs, hugs and kisses.

131

THIRTY-SIX

Gulping with tears and laughter, Sandie beckoned a stunned-looking Simon into her embrace as well. Duncan Fox rang a rope bell above the fireplace. As a semblance of composure eventually returned to the room, a servant carried in a silver tea service. Fox accepted the heavy tray from her and shut the door.

Sandie sat in the middle of the chaise longue with her arms wrapped tightly round both the twins. Simon emptied an inviting-looking armchair of books and newspapers, putting them on a nearby embroidered footstool. Duncan settled into a second armchair.

'So which of you painted the picture we travelled through?' asked Simon.

'I did,' Sandie said. 'I travelled here the night I disappeared, and brought the goblet with me. Then I painted it here, hoping you'd spot the clue. I took it back to the Abbey via another painting. It was risky, but it was the only thing I could think of at the time.'

Em couldn't stop staring at her mother. 'I can't believe we found you! We really found you!'

'I knew you would,' said Sandie. 'How long have I been gone from our time?'

'Almost two months,' said Simon.

Sandie looked appalled. She squeezed the twins even tighter. 'That was not my intention. You must know that.'

Duncan Fox was lighting a cigar, filling the room with pungent smoke. 'Emily,' he said, nodding at the tea service. 'Would you like to do the honours?'

After tea was served, Em did her best to fill her mother in on what had been happening. Matt listened in silence through most of the tea and the conversation. He stood up and wandered over to the window to think as Duncan Fox turned a tap on the length of rubber tubing next to the door. One by one, the impressive array of lamps flickered to life as he visited them. Outside on Raphael Terrace, Matt saw a man walking along the kerb of the pavement with a long pole, lighting the street lamps.

He was pleased that they had finally found their mum, truly he was. But finding her reminded him of the tensions lurking below the surface of their relationship. She had bound his dad in a painting. Matt couldn't escape that fact, no matter how happy he was that she was safe. Finding her here in 1848 just meant she had more secrets than ever.

Turning back to face his mother, he asked the question that had flashed through his mind the moment he had seen her dashing up the stairs.

'How did you get here in the first place, Mum?'

'Quite quickly after you were born,' Sandie said, 'I discovered that I could animate into paintings, travel to the time of their creation. Somehow my being pregnant with both of you triggered something dormant in my Animare DNA or . . . who knows? It doesn't matter.

'We were on the cusp of a new millennium. The Council of Guardians was tightening the rules, forcing more of our kind to go underground, to stay out of the public eye, to lie to each other about who and what we were. I could not reveal my time-travelling abilities to anyone.'

'Dad found out, didn't he?' asked Matt belligerently. 'So you had to get rid of him. You had to bind him in that painting.'

Sandie walked over to grip Matt's shoulders. 'It was nothing like that. I loved your dad, Mattie . . . in many ways I will always love your dad.' She lifted her hand and gently swept Matt's hair from his face. Her voice broke. 'You are so like him.'

THIRTY-SEVEN

You're such a . . . a jerk, Matt! Can't you see how you're upsetting her?

Em wrapped her arms around her weeping mother.

Fox rose from his chair, obviously uncomfortable with all the emotion. 'Sandie, I will carry the tea tray down to the parlour.'

Simon passed Sandie a handkerchief, as the artist headed for the door.

'We were living at the Abbey, as you know, Matt, having just celebrated your third birthdays,' Sandie continued, wiping her eyes. 'I was painting, your dad was researching, planning to write his definitive history of the Abbey and its art.' She looked up at Simon, 'And you, Simon, had just joined us with Zach.

'But Malcolm was terribly unhappy that we had gone into hiding after you two were born, and he was even angrier that his father Renard would not stand up to the Council of Guardians and their rules. Malcolm believed that with your powers, you—and he—could rule all the Councils of the world.'

'That's rubbish,' Matt snarled.

His head was pounding, his emotions tearing between relief that his mum was alive and anger that she had taken his dad from him all those years ago. He wanted to hug Sandie, to protect her and he wanted to . . . to . . . he wanted to scream.

'Matt,' Simon said, taking Matt's arm while dropping his voice and holding Matt's gaze. 'Son, walk it off . . . walk it all off.'

Matt began to circle the room slowly.

'One night after the Abbey was quiet, I found your dad poring over Duncan's diary,' Sandie went on. 'He had discovered it hidden in the vault. In the diary, Duncan explained that Hollow Earth truly existed, and wasn't a myth at all.'

'Renard showed us the diary earlier,' said Simon.

Sandie paused to dry her eyes. 'That night, your dad told me he knew that I could time-travel. He wanted me to go back and find out as much as possible about Hollow Earth. At first I thought he wanted the same things as Duncan did . . . does. But I came to realize that he wanted to use the beasts in Hollow Earth for his own purposes.'

'Why didn't you just leave?' asked Matt. 'Why did you have to bind him?'

'Because, Mattie—'

'Stop calling me that!'

'Because, Matt, your dad was manipulating your powers with his own inspiriting abilities, which are incredibly strong. He is Renard's son, after all. He planned to take you both from me. I caught him inspiriting you when you were just three years old, helping you animate yourselves into a painting . . . I could not let that happen again. Ever.'

Simon put his face in his hands. 'I wish I had known.'

'Simon, no one knew the depths to which Malcolm had already gone. Only Renard. And I made him swear on his honour as a Guardian and my friend to keep the secret.'

'And what about us?' asked Matt, his hands on his hips. 'When were you going to trust us enough to tell us?'

Sandie sighed. 'I was doing my best not to tell you any of this until you were older. I just wanted you both to be normal children.'

'Well,' said Em, her heart feeling lighter than it had in ages, 'we're having tea in Victorian London. I don't think there's much chance of normality any more.'

Sandie tugged Matt into her arms. For a few beats he resisted, then he let go.

THIRTY-EIGHT

Five minutes later, Duncan Fox returned to the studio, carrying an axe, a length of rope, a pair of opera glasses, four canteens of water and three changes of clothes. He set all of them on the chaise longue.

Simon's eyes widened. 'What's going on?'

'The children and Sandie are going back to 1263,' Duncan said.

Em looked up. They were going to the *Middle Ages*?

'You can't be serious,' said Simon in shock. 'To the monastery?'

'We have to, Simon,' said Sandie, pulling a cloak out of the pile and wrapping it around her shoulders. 'Em, Matt, change your clothes, please.'

'Why would you do such a stupid thing, especially when we've only just found you?' Simon demanded.

Em was already rifling through the clothing as if this was some kind of dressing-up game. She held up a pair of trousers that were so filthy they could stand by themselves, thick with the stench of boy sweat and stinky socks.

'These are all boys' clothes,' she said in disappointment. 'And they're disgusting.'

'I am sorry about that, Emily, but there was very little bathing happening in 1263,' said Duncan apologetically. 'And it will be safer for all involved if you travel as a boy.'

'They aren't going!' Simon said.

Ignoring the clothes, Matt wandered over to the windows. There was too much to think about. He slipped a piece of paper from his pocket and began to sketch the view in a bid to settle his nerves.

Em meanwhile settled on an only marginally offensive long-sleeved suede shirt that looked like a shift, and trousers that fastened with a belt of twine, and a shapeless cap. She picked up a brick of coal from the fire and, rubbing it in her hands, smeared the coal dust on her face and in her hair, muting the intensity of her neon streak.

'That's the spirit, young lady,' said Duncan, snatching up his sketchbook. He sat Em on the stool in front of the hearth and began to draw her portrait.

'I want an explanation,' Simon thundered.

'When the twins and I lived in London, I used to work at the Royal Academy,' Sandie said. 'One day I happened to be in the office of Sir Charles Wren, the head of the Council of Guardians, and discovered that he was gathering evidence about the Hollow Earth Society. Because of Malcolm's interest in Hollow Earth and his plans to use the twins to free the beasts inside, I looked at the evidence more closely. There was a key that particularly caught my attention, and I stole it.'

Simon pulled the rusty drawer key from his pocket. 'This key?'

Sandie nodded. 'Duncan's diary mentioned a key just like it. Malcolm wanted to find it. Because of Duncan's connection with Hollow Earth, I knew that it was likely to be the same key. So I travelled into one of Duncan's paintings at the Royal

139

Academy, to ask Duncan about it myself.'

'What happened when you met that first time?' asked Matt from the window, trying not to sound interested.

'I was across the street, sketching the front of the house last winter, trying to capture the play of the light and the shadows on the glass roof, when a woman shot out of my canvas in a shaft of brilliant light, knocking over the poor chimney sweep passing behind me,' Duncan said. 'I knew immediately she was an Animare. I hurried her quickly inside. We discovered the contents of my desk drawer together.'

'What was inside?' Em asked, glancing at the old desk in fascination.

'The first page of *The Book of Beasts*, sealed in wax paper where it had been hidden centuries ago.'

'How had it got there?'

'My builders recently uncovered that desk in a cedar chest filled with other pieces of furniture, hidden deep in the catacombs under the ruins of the Abbey,' said Duncan. 'I had no idea of its significance until I met your mother.'

'I came back here two months ago, through one of Duncan's paintings at the Abbey,' Sandie went on. 'And painted the picture that brought you here. I couldn't come home until I knew it was safe for all of us. But then Duncan and I uncovered something that meant I couldn't come home at all.'

THIRTY-NINE

'What did you uncover?' demanded Matt. He still hadn't touched the medieval clothes.

Duncan took up the story.

'My stonemasons discovered another priceless artefact in the catacombs. An incredibly well-preserved tapestry that has proven to be most useful to our research and your mother's travels. I have used it to make several painting trips. Only the other day, I found myself in an uncomfortable situation with one of our mutual ancestors.'

Sandie opened a chest in the corner of the room and lifted out what looked like a rolled-up rug. She carefully unfurled the tapestry along the sideboard. It showed several panels of life in a medieval monastery: monks at their high desks illustrating manuscripts, tilling the fields, getting on with their everyday life.

'It's beautiful,' commented Simon.

'Wow,' said Em in amazement. 'I can't believe how bright it is, after all these years.'

'That's because much of this was worked in gold threads,' said Duncan. 'As I am sure you know, gold doesn't tarnish. I've been using it to travel to the monastery in 1263, when the tapestry was made. And on one of my last visits with your mother, we discovered that a group of rebel monks is trying to open Hollow Earth.'

'We think we know how to stop them, but we

need the twins' help,' said Sandie, pleadingly. 'We have to go, Simon. Don't you see?'

Simon shook his head in frustration. 'I know I'm not your Guardian, Sandie, but I am your friend. You can't interfere. Whatever these so-called rebel monks are planning to do, they've already done it. Hollow Earth has not been unleashed on the world. We're all here. Monsters and demons are not roaming the earth. It's the twenty-first century— I mean, 1848. We can't change the past.'

'He's right, Mum,' Em agreed. 'In all the science fiction stories I've read, when a character changes the past, she always makes things worse.'

Sandie kissed her daughter's forehead. 'I appreciate your literary warning, but we have no choice. You see, I think we've already interrupted events. I think we have something to do with what's happening at the monastery in the Middle Ages.'

Duncan crumbled the end of his cigar into the ashes in the fire. 'On our last visit,' he said, 'we learned of a stranger who has appeared on the island and inflamed a handful of the monks, convincing them that their destiny lies in controlling the islands and opening Hollow Earth.'

'We cannot risk them finding the bone quill,' added Sandie. Even the soft tone of her voice couldn't disguise her disquiet.

'Grandpa told us about the quill,' said Matt. 'It's made from the antler of the black peryton, right?'

'And it opens Hollow Earth if an Animare uses it to copy illustrations from *The Book of Beasts*,' Simon said, nodding.

Sandie kneeled in front of Simon. 'I know this is a lot to ask,' she said, 'but I need your help. Duncan has travelled too often into the past. It's been taking its toll on him, and he's ill because of it. I can't do this by myself. If we go together—you, me and the children—our powers should be enough to do what must be done quickly, covertly and safely. If I go alone, I may not survive.'

FORTY

His mother's words were all Matt needed to hear. He'd lost her once. He had no intention of letting her out of his sight ever again.

He grabbed a handful of clothing and changed quickly. When he came back into the studio, he looked every bit the part of a medieval peasant, with his long, dark, wavy hair, a dirty, yellowing, long-sleeved undershirt, a leather waistcoat on top and scuffed black boots.

Duncan handed Matt the axe and Em the rope. 'I trust you will not need these items, but better to be prepared.' Then he gave each of them rolled-up sheets of paper with pencils slipped inside. 'These you may definitely need, but be discreet. This is a world without paper, a place of primitive needs and no luxuries.'

Simon had put on a cassock, which he was adjusting a little uncomfortably.

'You'll fit right in, Simon,' said Em, fiddling nervously with her own clothes.

Simon squeezed her hand, helping her keep her fears reined in. So far there had been no random acts of animation. He hoped Em could maintain her composure.

Em did too.

Sandie held Matt's and Em's eyes. 'If anything goes wrong, tear up your animation immediately and return here, then back to the Abbey in the 21st

145

century through the still-life.'

Simon adjusted his hood. The sackcloth scratched his neck. 'What exactly is the plan when we get to 1263?'

'Em and I will warn the Abbot of the threat to the islands and the Order,' said Sandie. 'Whatever or whoever is creating disquiet among the monks can't open Hollow Earth without using the bone quill and the unfinished manuscript of *The Book of Beasts*. But we cannot take either of the relics from their time. Doing that would cause untold chaos with the time continuum. We must simply warn the Abbot to move both the quill and the manuscript from the islands, at least until the threat has passed.'

'And what will Matt and I do while you two are warning the Abbot?' asked Simon.

'If I can't persuade him of the danger, I want you and Matt to steal the quill.'

'You know where it is?' asked Matt.

Duncan walked over to a sideboard in the corner of the studio next to the windows. Em recognized it as a piece of furniture in the flat downstairs, in her own time. He set a small book, the size of a diary, on a velvet pad on the top of the sideboard, and with great care opened it at the centre folio. 'This is one of the few remaining copies of the third Abbot's history of the monastery, up to 1214,' he said.

Everyone gathered around the sideboard. The pages were dull and cracked with age, and lacked the colour that distinguished the tapestry and the lone page from *The Book of Beasts*. The initial capital letter of the folio had a white-winged stag standing in the crossbar of the letter A in the

146

phrase 'A long time ago'.

'Why stop at 1214?' asked Matt, leaning over Em's shoulder to get a closer look. 'We want to know about 1263.'

'The third Abbot was burned at the stake that year. Accused of being a demon.'

'Oh,' said Matt. 'Not cool.'

Duncan looked at Matt with a strange expression. 'Of course it was not cool. In fact it would have been blistering hot.'

Em giggled. Matt started to explain his slang to Duncan, but Simon waved him off.

'In these pages are the creation story of the island and how in the beginning there were two perytons,' said Duncan.

'We know that,' said Em. 'Grandpa told us. Two perytons, one black and one white.'

'Correct. According to this ancient book, all that was left of the black peryton when it fell into the frozen north was a section of its antler. One of the first Animare in those icy lands carved the antler into a quill. When the Animare died at a great age, according to the chronicle, a small band of monks from Era Mina stole the bone quill and returned it to the islands.'

Matt was fascinated by the tale, but even more taken with the lush lettering of the words on the folio. The closer he looked, the more the words seemed to sing to him, the story filling his head like the melody from a favourite song.

'The bone quill was buried in the tomb of the third Abbot, the one burned at the stake,' said Duncan, closing the manuscript and returning it to a glass container in the sideboard. 'And that is where you must go in order to find it.'

Matt picked up the axe, swinging it dangerously above his head. 'So Simon and I are going to get some tomb-raider action?' he said. 'Awesome.'

Shaking his head, Simon yanked the axe from Matt's hands.

'I'll animate first and take Em with me directly to the Abbot.' Sandie pointed to one of the middle panels on the tapestry. 'Most of this tapestry was imagined in the great hall of the monastery, where it was spread on wooden scaffolds while the monks sketched and stitched, but it was hung in the Abbot's tower. Because of that, I can't control exactly where we'll come through. We may get separated when we do.'

'I'm not happy with this plan at all,' Simon muttered, setting the axe on the floor.

'I know,' said Em, squeezing his hand. 'I can tell.'

'We'll try our best to convince the Abbot to remove both the book and the bone quill from the islands while you and Matt search the catacombs,' Sandie told Simon.

'Great,' said Matt. 'We get a creepy dungeon and Em gets a library.'

'Probably just as well,' replied Simon, 'given what Em's fears might animate.'

Sandie pocketed a spiral notebook with a pen clipped to its binding. Matt handed the sketch that had brought them here to Duncan, who rolled it up and slipped it inside the mouth of the skull on the old desk.

'It will be there when you return,' he said, 'in the event that I am not.'

Em gave Duncan a hug. 'Thank you for taking care of our mum.'

'You're welcome, my dear.'

Em hooked her arm in her mother's as Sandie started sketching. Simon gripped Matt's undershirt as Matt did the same. Two pictures of the centre panel in the tapestry began to illuminate.

FORTY-ONE

The Abbey
Present Day

In the Abbey's library, it was close to midnight. Renard, Jeannie and Zach were up late, playing a long, slow game of *The Settlers of Catan*. After moving one of his armies, Zach spotted the particles of light above the still-life explode into bright stars of white light and then fade to the faintest glimmer.

'What do ye think just happened, Mr R?' asked Jeannie.

'I wish I knew,' said Renard heavily. 'I wish I knew.'

PART THREE

FORTY-TWO

The Monastery of Era Mina
Middle Ages

Hunched over his desk, the Abbot was struggling with thorny choices—decisions that the first monks of the Order had also had to make when faced with insurrection, and monks wanting to use their powers in unsanctioned ways.

Solon's battle with the Grendel in Skinner's Bog the previous night had not gone unnoticed in the imaginations of the monastery's Guardians. One or two of them had experienced such anguish when the fight was at its most intense that they had locked themselves in their cells and refused to come out. Although he didn't yet know the details, the Abbot's Guardian talents meant that he knew enough. He knew about the Grendel's attack.

The Grendel had always been the beast that lurked closest to the world of men, and it was the last creature from ancient times that the monks needed to draw into *The Book of Beasts*. If only Brother Renard hadn't damaged himself to the point where the book could no longer be finished! Freeing the peryton had been a terrible mistake. It had weakened the Order's control over Hollow Earth, and roused the Grendel from its slumber. By animating the peryton, Brother Renard had achieved nothing but a fleeting victory against the

Norsemen, who were likely to come again, and soon. Releasing the peryton from Hollow Earth might have started a chain of events that even the Abbot struggled to imagine. Releasing the peryton might have awakened the island itself. God help them all if that were true.

The Abbot pushed the unfinished *Book of Beasts* aside and dipped his quill in the ink well, tapping the nib against the side of the clay pot and letting the black liquid settle in the shaved point. He returned to the task of the Abbey's accounts, hoping the tedious copying from one register to another would distract him from his worries.

The list of the monthly tithes from the farms was growing, the monastery's accumulating wealth becoming a matter of concern. Whenever money gathered in one place, violence surely followed. The monks might have built a self-sustaining community on these islands, but they had not completely cut themselves off from the world.

The Abbot sighed, noting the ink had smudged on the line of figures he'd been dawdling over. Reaching across his desk, he grabbed a square of cheesecloth to clean up his spill.

The colourful tapestry that covered most of the wall behind the Abbot's desk shifted slightly in the wind battering the shutters. The carpet of cloth blazed with illumination, threads of gold, red and black creating a stunning history of the monastery in large, stitched panels. It was the Abbot's own masterpiece, a work that he had imagined on woodblocks and smaller parchment before finally finishing, tying the closing knots on the final panel in a bid to soothe his mind while Solon battled in the bog.

The Abbot ran his calloused fingers across the rough knots of thread on the reverse side of the cloth. He prayed that it would not be the last legacy he might ever leave.

Rising from his chair—a high-backed wooden throne carved with the Abbey's coat of arms—the Abbot walked across to the shuttered window. He peered through the slats at the storm slipping slowly over the island. Out there in the darkness, the rocky cliffs and peaks of the islands were pocked with unlit bonfires. When set alight, the fires created a chain running the length of the Western Isles, calling men to arms against any invading armies.

But what, thought the Abbot, if the enemy came from within the Abbey itself?

FORTY-THREE

The darkness! The black peryton's shadow . . . It is seeping towards us.

The darkness of which Brother Renard spoke in his story of the twin perytons and the perils tied to the unfinished *Book of Beasts* was close. Solon had been sensing it for days. And now he had witnessed two of his trusted brothers desecrating the sacred crypt and talking as if they wished him dead. Who was this prophet they spoke of? What was the significance of the bone quill they were seeking? And why did they want *The Book of Beasts*? He had to speak to the Abbot about all of it.

The water had receded a little. Solon waded across the flooded courtyard in the descending darkness. Pushing open the heavy wooden doors, he lifted a torch hanging in an iron bracket above him, and climbed the steep stairs of the Abbot's tower.

*   *   *

A loud knock shook the door. In a rush, the Abbot grabbed *The Book of Beasts* from his desk and slid it into the hidden compartment behind the coat of arms in his high-backed chair. He did not notice the first page fluttering from the folio and under his desk.

'Enter,' he said.

A draught of cold air rushed into the chamber, followed by a dirty and dishevelled Solon.

'I am glad to see that you survived your mission to Skinner's Bog, Solon,' said the Abbot. 'I sensed your struggles and the terrible strength of the Grendel. You retrieved the berries?'

Solon nodded breathlessly. 'I'm sorry I didn't come earlier, Father Abbot. I . . . I needed to sleep and then I lost all sense of time today.'

'Brother Cornelius dressed your wounds, I see,' said the Abbot. 'I sensed someone else with you—a girl?'

'A Viking girl, master. She was badly injured. Brother . . . Brother Cornelius said that he would see to her wounds.'

'Quickly, close the door. You're bringing the storm in here with you.' The Abbot waved Solon to a stool. 'Did this Viking girl tell you anything that might be useful to us? Is another attack as imminent as the naysayers among the brothers seem to think?'

'Only that the Norsemen left her for dead.'

'Is she a young woman the minstrels may one day sing about?' the Abbot inquired.

Solon blushed and nodded. The Abbot smiled kindly.

'And I have sensed that she has faculties that suggest she may be one of us?'

Solon nodded again. 'It surprised me, sir,' he said. 'I was not aware that girls could be like us in that way.'

'It is quite unusual to find a girl with our imaginative gifts,' said the Abbot. 'I daresay there are more among us than we will ever discover. For it is far too easy for a girl or a woman with our

157

faculties to be dismissed as a witch or worse. The price they must pay is far too high.'

'Please, Father Abbot,' said Solon in a rush, 'I am grateful for your interest, but my visit here tonight carries great urgency. The unfinished manuscript, *The Book of Beasts*, is it safe?'

The Abbot looked startled by the question. 'It is hidden,' he said. 'Why—'

At that moment, the door blew open and then just as quickly slammed closed. Startled, the Abbot and Solon looked around. There was no one inside or outside the room.

And yet . . . a chill lingered, swirling round them. The Abbot shivered, rubbing his arms for warmth. He felt the atmosphere in the room changing. An animation, a creation from another powerful imagination was forming nearby.

'Solon,' he said, panic rising in his voice, 'whatever is coming, it must not find the island's secrets.'

A squall of wind snapped open the shutters, lifting the tapestry off the wall with such force that it flew up towards the beamed ceiling. When it unfurled, two bodies—a woman and a boy—toppled out, covered in a webbing of red, black and golden threads.

FORTY-FOUR

At first Solon was too stunned to move. The lines of interlacing light covering the woman and the boy were like a giant spider's web. He jolted to his senses when the Abbot exclaimed, 'By God in the heavens! Who are you?'

'My name is Sandie Calder, sir, and this is my daughter, Emily. We are Animare.'

'Daughter?' asked Solon in astonishment, taking in the girl's clothes.

The woman brushed the dust off her dress and helped the girl disentangle herself from the tapestry. Solon offered the girl his hand to help her off the ground, while the Abbot assisted the woman.

'Were you hiding in the rafters?' asked Solon, staring up at the heavy wooden beams, then back at the girl, his eyes wide.

'Not exactly,' said the girl, adjusting her tunic.

Her cap was on the floor. Solon picked it up and handed it over. 'Is your coloured hair a mark of your clan?' he asked curiously.

'In a way,' said the girl, accepting the hat.

'We don't have much time to explain,' said the woman, 'but our future needs your help.'

*   *   *

The Abbot listened closely to Sandie's story about

a force from the future infiltrating the monastery, intent on stealing the bone quill and *The Book of Beasts*. As absurd as Sandie's story sounded, given the rising disquiet among the Order, and recent thefts of food from the kitchen, the Abbot was inclined to believe her. The emotions he was reading from her served to support the tale.

'What can I do to help?' he asked at last.

'I know that you will not give up the bone quill or *The Book of Beasts*. I don't expect that from you,' said Sandie. 'These are your sacred relics, symbols of your ancient past, and they should remain part of this world. But I am asking that you send them from the islands until you find the person or the thing that lurks here out of time.'

'Solon,' said the Abbot. 'Find our guests two strong mugs of mead and stoke the fire. I must consult with Brother Cornelius on this matter. I will return with a decision shortly.'

Solon looked dismayed. 'Master, there is more that I must tell—'

But the Abbot had already shut the door.

The storm had shifted inland, leaving choppy waters lapping at the steps of many of the monastery buildings. Waves were crashing against the monastery's outer walls too, sending even more dampness seeping through the mortar.

Before finding Brother Cornelius, the Abbot felt an urge to check on the safety of the bone quill. Tugging his hood over his head, he pushed into the wind, half-running and half-walking through the covered cloisters, not stopping until he reached a section of the wall where the bricks shimmered subtly as if shafts of moonlight were illuminating them, their corners furling and unfurling like the

160

arms of a starfish.

Standing in front of this section of bricks, the Abbot took a key from inside his wide sleeve and slid it into the midsection of the bricks. Instantly, a small, arched, wooden door shielded behind an animation was revealed.

Ducking his head, the Abbot went into the passageway behind the door. Twenty steps in, he turned into a tunnel on his left that opened up into the chamber of the crypts.

The chamber was awash with the yellow light of a flaming torch and thick with the iron smell of blood. Brother Cornelius's broken body lay on the top of the first martyr's tomb, two gold coins covering his eyes. They glimmered at the Abbot with the grotesque illusion of life.

Bile rushed to the Abbot's mouth. He ran to the farthest corner of the chamber and vomited. He remained crouched there for a long time, praying. Then he wiped his mouth on his sleeve and forced himself to take stock of the rest of the chamber.

The lines running through the sand on the stony ground suggested more than one scuffle had occurred here recently. Averting his eyes from poor Brother Cornelius, the Abbot gaped at the desecrated bodies of the mummies. Finally, he detected the worst horror of all in this sacred space.

The bone quill was gone.

FORTY-FIVE

Matt and Simon were not so lucky, animating through the tapestry directly into the rising tide outside the kitchens, the lashing rain and gale-force wind slashing against their exposed skin.

Pulling himself on to his feet, Matt looked around for Simon. The older man was in much deeper water, wading towards him. His cassock looked as if it weighed a hundred kilos. The two of them climbed up the rocky shoreline and collapsed.

'Well,' said Matt, spitting seaweed from his mouth, 'that was no fun.'

'I am not dragging this much weight around,' said Simon, stripping off his cassock to the jeans and T-shirt he still wore underneath. He held his hand out to Matt. 'Let's get to shelter, try to dry off and figure out how to get down to the catacombs.'

The two of them sloshed into the outbuilding nearest where they had materialized. Skinned rabbits and deer hung from the rafters, sharing space with flocks of de-feathered pigeons.

'Oh, man,' said Matt, 'an abattoir? I'm not hanging out . . . sorry . . . staying in here.'

The next building better suited their needs. With wide wooden doors that could be open or closed depending on the weather, it held a hearth big enough for even Simon to stand inside. The fire was raging and three heavy iron pots hanging from hooks at chimney height were bubbling and steaming. The fuggy warmth was bliss.

Em, can you hear me?

Yes! Where are you guys?

I think we're in one of the kitchens, close to the water, which is where we landed. We need dry clothes or we're going to freeze to death.

Mum and I are at the top of the Abbot's tower. Our swimming pool is built over its foundations. The Abbot's really nice, although very confused. There's a totally hot boy, too.

Great. So glad you've met a boy. Focus, Em. Ask Mum how we can get some clothes.

Simon dragged two stools as close to the fire as possible and was ladling thick yellow broth from one of the pots into wooden bowls. Holding one bowl up to his face, he inhaled the warmth.

'You were just talking to Em in your head, right? Where are they?' he asked, passing Matt a bowl of the broth.

'In one of the towers with the Abbot and a cute boy.'

Simon laughed. 'I'm glad they came through safely.'

The broth smelled delicious, and Matt realized he was really hungry. But given what he'd just seen hanging in the abattoir, he wasn't sure he was going to let any of this liquid pass his lips.

'Drink up,' said Simon. 'It's leeks and turnips. It won't kill you.'

Mum says draw dry clothes.

And so Matt did. Problem was, he knew nothing about the fashions of the Middle Ages. All he could think of were his favourite movies set in medieval times.

'Think leggings, leather boots, tunics,

waistcoats,' said Simon. 'Nothing flashy, but I'd appreciate some dry boxers, please.'

'No way am I animating you a pair of boxers,' said Matt.

'Fair enough,' said Simon, warming himself at the blazing fire. 'But your mum's idea to animate dry clothes was a good one. They'll give off a sheen of light, which we'll need, since we don't have any torches. But we should hurry. Someone's bound to return to this building soon.'

Matt finished his soup, then set about animating outfits for each of them. Simon's dry clothes shot from the paper to his feet in streamers of swirling grey light, while Matt's appeared on his lap in a tower of coloured rectangles, dropping one on top of the other, largest to smallest.

When the storm subsided, Simon and Matt went outside to investigate the other buildings, looking like glow-in-the-dark characters from Monty Python's *Holy Grail*.

It didn't take them long to find the door to the catacombs tucked away in the last of the three kitchen buildings. Several casks of wine had been rolled away from where they had been blocking the door.

'Let's just go down,' said Matt. 'We can scout around and then when we get Mum's go-ahead to find the quill, we'll already be on the spot.'

Simon slid down the wall to the floor. 'We wait here, Matt,' he said, sounding shattered. 'The less interference we can cause to this time, the better.'

'Are you okay?' asked Matt, joining Simon against the wall.

'I'm thinking time-travel may have an adverse effect on anyone over forty.'

'Doesn't everything have an adverse effect on anyone over forty?' said Matt, grinning.

'Watch it, buddy,' said Simon. 'I'm serious. I'm exhausted. No wonder Duncan can't travel any more. I feel as if I've inspirited a crowd of people and I've been awake for days.'

'More like centuries.'

Matt! Can you hear me?

Matt sat up. *What's wrong?*

Everything.

Simon was dozing. Matt nudged him awake. 'It's Mum and Em. We have to go.'

Mum says we're too late. Someone's already stolen the bone quill and murdered one of the monks. The Abbot just came back from the catacombs. He's really upset. Mum says meet us on the hillside behind the Abbot's tower right away. Stay away from the main buildings.

Matt and Simon hastily made sure they had left no trace in the kitchen of their presence. Then they sprinted outside, along the garden path. When two monks, heads bowed in deep conversation, came walking towards them, they ducked into the woods, cutting through the trees and up the hillside behind the tower. The partially built walls of the tower on Era Mina loomed at them across the bay.

FORTY-SIX

'There they are,' said Em, spotting the faint ethereal glow from Simon's and Matt's clothing as they jogged through the trees.

Sandie hiked her dress and her cloak up under her arms and followed Em to the top of the hill.

'Em, stop!' she hissed, when they were halfway to the top. 'Did you hear something?'

Em stopped and listened. She could hear the last gasp of the storm rustling through the white birch and the spindly pine trees, spraying the ground with rain from the branches when it did, and she could hear the waves crashing against the shore directly beneath them.

'I don't hear anything unusual,' she said, taking two more steps up the hillside.

And then she did. A low, feral growling.

'What is that?'

Sandie looked pale. 'I don't know . . . but faster, Em. Faster.'

When they reached the place where Matt and Simon were crouched behind thick briar bushes, they were breathless, and the hem of Sandie's dress was filthy.

'Did you hear the growling?' Simon asked.

Em and Sandie nodded.

'Why did we have to get out of the monastery so fast?' asked Matt, as Sandie ripped the bottom half of her dress away so that she could move her legs more easily.

'The Abbot is afraid the rebel monks may be taking over the monastery tonight.'

'You mean like a coup?' asked Matt.

Sandie nodded. 'The Abbot told us to hide in one of the empty cottages on the other side of the island, but I think we need to return to the present. Get Renard's advice. Figure out what to do next. We're not prepared to take this on if the rebel monks already have the quill.'

'Did you ask the Abbot about getting the quill and the book off the island?' asked Simon, using the opera glasses Duncan had given them to scan the dark monastery and its outer buildings tucked in the forest beneath them.

'He was retrieving the quill from its hiding place when he discovered a murdered monk.'

Another keening howl, a blood-curdling sound, shook the ground beneath them. Em screamed. Matt scowled at her, then looked down at the monastery buildings.

Two black double-headed hellhound gargoyles were growing out from the monastery wall in a strobe of white light. Two monks stood illuminated on the nearest parapet, one in a stunning purple robe and the other in a plain brown sackcloth cassock. Both had their cowls over their heads, the wind from the passing storm barely shifting the cloth.

With bone-chilling howls, the hellhounds wrenched themselves from the stone and headed directly towards the twins, Sandie and Simon. 'Run!' screamed Sandie.

FORTY-SEVEN

The hounds galloped up the hillside, their grotesque heads more mountain lion than dog, the scent of Animare sending them into a frenzy. Their paws slapped the ground like drums of war, and their sabre teeth snapped loud enough to rustle starlings and cormorants from the trees. Their nostrils flared smoke, their eyes burned, and their black coats trailed white-hot flames.

The four of them sprinted down the other side of the hill, Matt in the lead, Simon close by, and Em and Sandie directly behind them.

'Get out the drawing of Duncan's tapestry, Matt,' yelled Sandie. 'When you and Simon get to the beach, tear yours up.'

Matt lost his footing so many times, he gave up and gave in to gravity, sliding down through the undergrowth, branches smacking at his face when he couldn't duck fast enough.

Sandie and Em were holding hands, balancing each other against the rough terrain. Sandie's dress caught on a buried tree branch, slowing the two of them even more.

'Can't we draw something?' screamed Em.

'No time, Em,' her mum panted. 'Those beasts are coming too fast.'

The hellhounds broke through the line of trees at the top of the hill. Pausing for a beat at the cusp of the hill, they raised their steaming snouts

168

into the cold wind, letting out a keening howl that carried forever in the wind, as they caught the scent of their terrified prey.

Matt was ahead of everyone. He turned in time to see the lead hound pounce into the air, its body the size of a Siberian tiger.

Em! Look out!

Em let go of her mum's hand, whipped the knife Duncan had given her from the band of her tunic and pivoted on the rocky ground just as the beast came down on top of her. Squeezing her eyes closed, Em lunged, shoving the blade deep into its chest. Instead of the animation exploding in light and colour, the hellhound fractured into shards that froze above Em's head for a second and then began to reassemble.

Neither Em nor Sandie waited to see the result. Sandie grabbed Em's hand and dragged her on down the hillside.

'Don't look back!' yelled Simon to Matt. 'Keep going!'

Em couldn't help it. She turned and saw the reformed hellhound flying over the undergrowth again with every leap and bound. Her heart was racing, her face bleeding from whipping branches. Her legs were like rubber.

She wasn't going to make it.

'Whose animation is this?' Matt shouted at Simon.

'I don't know!' yelled Simon.

The second hellhound had taken a liking to Matt. It was almost running parallel with him, its two heads cocked as if taunting Matt with its speed, the flames from its back searing Matt's tunic. Up ahead, Matt spotted a narrow path through a copse of hawthorn trees. If he hit the incline correctly, he could kick-flip over the undergrowth and gain a little distance.

Matt squeezed his eyes closed and thought of the incline as his skateboard. He hit the hard ground and went into a tight flip, somersaulting over the brush and landing on his feet on the hard sand, seconds before the hound. Simon broke through the woods a few metres further down the hill, sprinting over the rocks towards Matt.

On the hillside, Sandie and Em were trying desperately to get to the beach. Simon's hand was already gripping Matt's arm. Matt had his drawing out, ready to tear it up. The hound was readying itself to pounce on both of them.

And then, out of the darkness, from the Abbot's tower came a volley of fiery arrows slicing through the sky towards Matt and Simon. Simon shoved Matt to the ground, throwing himself on top of him. Two arrows, one splitting the shaft of the other, pierced Simon's shoulder, the flames collapsing into ash when they hit Simon's back.

'Tear up your drawing, Matt!' screamed Sandie, a hundred yards behind them. 'We'll be right behind you!'

Blood was gushing from Simon's shoulder.

'I'll be okay, Matt,' gasped Simon, calming the boy's terror. 'When we get home, the arrows will vanish.'

'What about the wound?'

'A few stitches will sort it. Do what your mum says. We need to get back to the Abbey. Em and your mum will follow us.'

The hound now stood on four massive, flaming paws on a flat rock in front of Matt. Thick green spit frothed from its two mouths, flying at Simon and Matt. When a blob hit Matt's arm, it burned into his skin. Matt yelped and ripped it off, noticing a puddle-shaped tattoo of green left on his bleeding arm.

The other hound was at Em's heels, its hot breath singeing her ankles, sabre teeth snagging the skin on her leggings. Em's legs were cramping as she raced onwards. She was really not going to make it. She tried to swallow back her tears, but they came anyway.

Sandie's drawing was inside the bodice of her dress. She pulled it out, waving at Matt that she was ready.

'Tear up your drawing!' she screamed at Matt again. 'We'll follow with ours. When you get to 1848, use the picture in the skull's mouth to get home. Don't worry about us.'

Sandie knew the picture she'd painted to take her to 1848 in the first place was still in Fox's studio.

The two-headed hound snapped at the back of Em's legs, taking a chunk out of her calf. She dropped to her knees in pain, sliding forward on her stomach.

Their panicked running had shifted them away from the beach, and the ground was rising again. A rocky cliff-edge lay ahead of them. Em pushed her mother violently over the top.

Matt, tear up your picture, DO IT!

Simon grabbed the drawing from Matt's hands and tore it up.

FORTY-EIGHT

The Abbey
Present Day

Simon and Matt skated along a shimmering wave of light from the still-life into the Abbey library. Simon landed clumsily on his side. The wound on his back was still bleeding, but the animated arrows had vanished. Matt managed to land on his feet, took three hops and slammed into two chairs.

Renard, Jeannie and Zach were sitting at the fire, all three dozing, wrapped in their dressing gowns and pyjamas, their feet resting on the hearth. Jeannie bolted up and dashed from the library in search of her first-aid kit.

'Thank God you're all okay—' Renard's voice changed. 'Where's Em?'

Simon was staggering to his feet when Matt charged at him, screaming and knocking him back against a table.

'You left them! How could you leave them!' He pounded on Simon's chest, worsening the wound on his back. Simon grabbed Matt's wrists as the boy yelled again. 'And you tore up the picture in the skull's mouth!'

'Your mum is with Em, Matt. We were about to be mauled to death! You heard your mother— there's another picture they can use to get home. Look at me, son—'

172

'I'm not your son,' yelled Matt. 'If I was, then maybe you wouldn't have left your daughter behind!'

'Where is Em?' Zach signed urgently.

'He left them. He left them! Simon tore up my drawing. I could feel that Em wasn't coming. I sensed she was not coming,' Matt wailed. 'He left Mum there, too.'

Renard's eyes widened in shock. With a gasp, Jeannie stopped at the door, her hands full of medical supplies.

'Turns out Sandie shares the twins' ability to time-travel through paintings.' Simon coughed, doubling over in pain. 'She's been hiding out in 1848 with Fox, travelling with him to the Abbey in the Middle Ages to find the rest of *The Book of Beasts* and the bone quill. She was hoping that the Abbot . . .'

Simon slumped against Renard and passed out.

'I need to go back,' said Matt, frantically looking around for paper and a pencil. 'We can't leave them there. Rebel monks have taken control of the islands. They need my help!'

Zach grabbed Matt's shoulders and forced him on to a chair. Matt slumped where he sat, head in his hands, finally too exhausted to argue or fight any more. He started laughing instead.

Outside, the rain and wind pelted against the tall windows as if the storm had followed them across the centuries, while Renard and Jeannie helped the semi-conscious Simon up the stairs to bed. The security spotlights were flooding the grounds, white-capped waves crashing on to the beach. The island's protective shield turned the water into silver, white and black ink, dripping down the wall like a Jackson Pollock painting.

Matt was still laughing.

'What the hell's so funny?' Zach signed, angry and upset.

'The burn on my arm! How do I explain to a doctor that I've been gobbed on by a myth?' Matt finally got a frantic grip on himself. 'We need to go back, Zach. Hollow Earth will open if the rebel monks also get their hands on *The Book of Beasts*. Em and Mum can't be there when that happens.'

'Matt, you're exhausted,' Renard observed, coming back into the room. 'Simon's shoulder is wounded and Zach is in no position to go on his own. Jeannie's talents are not only in her cooking. She trained as a nurse many years ago. She'll stitch up Simon's wound and then fix up your burn as good as new. I promise. Then you need to heal, and we need to prepare ourselves. Now that we know what we're up against, we can prepare.'

FORTY-NINE

Half an hour later, Jeannie marched into the kitchen in her blood-spattered dressing gown with Simon's soiled T-shirt in her hands. She tossed the shirt into the laundry basket.

'Your father will be fine, Zach,' she signed, as Zach filled the kettle. 'A cup of tea would be grand, son, but first let's look at that injury of yours, Matt.'

Matt shifted off the corner of the couch to let Jeannie sit close to the hearth. The Abbey may have been updated and modernized down the years, but underneath all the caulk and central heating it was still a big draughty old castle in its bones. He held out his injured arm for Jeannie to examine.

'That's nasty,' said Jeannie at last. 'Burning saliva from a hellhound, I'll warrant?'

Matt shrugged. Jeannie put her warm, calloused hand on his knee. 'Son, I know you're hurting, but your grandpa is right. None of you is in any condition tonight to charge back into the Middle Ages.'

After Matt's wound was dressed, Jeannie took off her slippers, holding her thick-stockinged feet as close to the flames as she could without melting her toes.

'How bad is Dad, Jeannie?' signed Zach.

'He'll be fine. I've given him something to help him sleep, so he'll be out for a while. I've stitched up the wound.' She reached into her dressing gown pocket and pulled out a plastic bag. 'But I thought you might like to have this.'

She handed a segment of a flint arrowhead to Zach.

'Thanks.' Looking sick, Zach stared at the thing that had come centimetres from stealing his dad from him. Then, putting it down on the table, he went to the cooker to silence the keening kettle.

Matt picked up the sharpened flint. 'How can this have remained, if the arrows disappeared?'

'I don't know, Matt,' Renard admitted. 'I've never experienced anything like it.'

'Maybe,' said Jeannie, setting out the milk and sugar, 'it's the combination of being caught in Simon's shoulder and the power of the weans' time-travel abilities.'

Renard, Jeannie and Matt launched into a discussion of time-travel and its many unknowns. Zach was still dealing with the kettle. Matt switched off and thought about what might be happening to his mum and Em. The longer he sat in front of this cosy hearth in comfort and safety, the deeper his worries grew. He felt sick.

'Calm yourself, my boy,' said Renard softly.

Matt knew he was being inspirited but he was too tired to resist. Besides, his Guardian abilities did not yet equal his powers as an Animare. But before his rage had completely evaporated, he had one last thought.

If they wouldn't help him save Em and his mum, he'd find someone who would.

FIFTY

Much later that night, Matt lay awake in bed. The shadows on the ceiling were mocking him. No matter which way he looked, he could see Em in the shapes darting across his bedroom wall, and he could see his mum in the elongated figures folded in the swaying curtains. Pulling the duvet over his head, he squeezed his eyes closed.

It didn't help.

His arm throbbed with every toss and turn. It was inevitable that the hellhounds had caught his mum and Em. Perhaps even torn them to pieces. Even if they had survived, the monks had them now. What would they do to them?

Matt kicked off the duvet. He was too hot. He was too tired. He was too tense. He dragged his hands through his hair, rubbing at the sharp pain behind his eyes. Then he climbed from his bed and pulled open the curtains.

The lawn was brightly lit by the security lights, while the pulsing light from the tower on Era Mina flashed across the rest of the island's wind-blown landscape. The rain had stopped, but the wind was howling, battering the small island with waves.

Is it stormy where you are, Em?

His twin sister loved nights like this. She would listen to the crashing sea, imagining the waves rising up as beautiful sirens calling to her. Matt swiped his hand across his eyes. He would not cry.

177

He went over to the desk where he'd left his sketchpad and folder stuffed with a couple of the old maps and ancient prints that he'd been looking at in the library before they'd gone into the still-life.

Switching on his desk lamp, Matt sat and flipped through the folder with the maps and sketches. He noticed one that he hadn't paid much attention to before. It looked like a set of plans for the construction of the monastery and its catacombs.

Dragging the light closer, he knocked over his parents' wedding photograph, which he kept framed on his desk. He set it carefully upright again. Then he turned back to the drawing.

He traced his fingers along the smudged ink lines of the catacombs running beneath the monastery, noticing that the tunnels formed an Apostles' cross with soft clover-leaf shapes at the end of each arm. Matt guessed that one of those clover-leaves had held the crypt where the Abbot had discovered the murdered monk and the loss of the quill.

The main tunnel started from the south wing of the Abbey, which had been converted in the last twenty years to a swimming pool. It passed under the lawn and the main part of the building, ending beneath Renard's tower at another clover-leaf that today, Matt knew, held the art vault.

An idea began to form. He took the plans of the tunnels and climbed back into his bed to think it through. Suddenly, thoughts of rescuing his mother and sister changed from an abstract notion to a tangible plan.

FIFTY-ONE

The Monastery of Era Mina
Middle Ages

The hellhound sat back on its massive haunches, taking the position it normally held on the monastery's balustrade. Its steaming breath smelled of rotten eggs and burnt leaves, its inky black coat covered in a sticky tar-like substance. The hound bared both sets of sabre teeth at Em, a growl rising from deep in its body.

As soon as she felt in her mind that Matt had torn up the drawing, Em had thrown herself into a hollowed-out tree and shimmied her back up against the curving shell of the trunk, her knees pulled up to her chin. The hellhound made no attempt to reach its massive paw into the hole and drag her out.

'Em! Can you hear me?' called Sandie hysterically. She had scrambled free from the bracken that had cushioned her fall and was running back up the hill. 'The others have gone! The hound that was chasing them has gone, too!'

'I'm inside a tree,' yelled Em, relieved that she was not alone. 'But I can't get out. The stupid hound has me trapped.'

She could hear loud rustling coming closer. It came into her mind that whoever had animated the hounds was coming down the hillside. She had to

179

get out of here.

Digging into her tunic pocket, Em pulled out the pad and the pencil that Duncan had given her before they left his studio and began to draw.

As she sketched, a beam of light unrolled like a blind over the opening of the hollow in the tree and covered it completely. At the same time, a similar light rolled up the other side of the tree, creating a new opening for Em to crawl through. The hound remained immobile, as if it had already turned to stone, its black coat shimmering from the light of its animation and the harvest moon drifting from the storm clouds overhead.

Em's animation had come at a price. A figure with a crossbow over his shoulders scrambled down the hill, heading straight for the light. Em felt trapped, unable to run. The only choice was to attack. It went against her nature, but with a strength and fury she didn't know she had, she began to kick and scratch, taking the monk by surprise. But just as it looked as if Em might be managing to punch and squirm her way to freedom, the hound suddenly let out an earth-shaking howl and sprang on top of her, pinning her shoulders to the hillside.

'Mum! Help! Help!' But Sandie had vanished.

The heat from the hound's wet breath was blistering the skin on Em's neck, yet she couldn't move no matter how hard she struggled. Fire burned in the beast's eyes. Em could see her own reflection in the flames. Terror thickened her blood, tightening her muscles, making her head pound and her shoulders ache against the pressing weight of the slobbering monster.

'Mum? Where are you?' Em screamed.

180

How could this be happening?

The hound tipped its heads to the moon and howled. The more she fought against it, the more it appeared to solidify in front of her eyes. Em shivered with fear and pain, exhaustion and defeat.

Fear.

That's it, Em thought. *Let my fears loose.*

She forced herself to stare into the beast's eyes, to allow her panic to build as the monster met her gaze. Her heart raced. Her mouth felt as if she had swallowed sand. She let go.

At first, nothing happened. Then a fireball the size of a melon shot from the top of a nearby pine tree, exploding at the feet of the monk. He screamed and leaped away from the burst of flames.

A volley of fireballs followed instantly from the first one, shooting from the trees like flaming hailstones. One hit the haunches of the hellhound, igniting a line of flames up its legs and along its spine to both its heads.

That one had been a bit too close.

Em tried to turn her head away from the crowns of flame now white-hot on the top of the hound's heads, but she couldn't. Her face was reddening from the heat, her skin burning, burning . . .

Control, Em, she reminded herself hysterically. *Get your fears under control before this forest becomes an inferno.*

But the fireballs persisted. The trees lifted their branches into the darkness like limbs and lobbed fire in every shape and size, while the monk danced around the hound in a desperate attempt to stamp out the blaze. His efforts were in vain.

Em's eyes were smarting from the smoke that

had erupted from the thick, brambly undergrowth around them. The monk yelled as he batted a fireball back up into the trees like a cricket ball. Then he jumped on top of a crackling, spitting band of flames curling across the ground like a—

Python, thought Em involuntarily.

At once, a fiery python's head lunged from the blaze, its pink, fleshy mouth wide enough to swallow a man, its hooked fangs the size of a dragon's claws. It hissed and sent flames sparking across the monk's robes. Howling in a frenzy, the monk stripped off his robe, hopping in tattered and filthy long johns as he beat out the flames with his cassock.

Almost the entire hillside was engulfed in flames, when out of the thicket above them, a second monk appeared. Trying not to panic about the ring of fire all around her, Em noticed the figure's commanding air.

With long, dark hair draping a face already shrouded beneath his cowl, this monk let his gaze fall on Em. His stare felt like a cold hand squeezing her heart. Despite the burning heat, Em shivered uncontrollably. Without a word, the monk looked away, and she felt the power of the flames once again.

Even in the distorting light from the fire and the light from the moon, Em could see this monk's robe was more elaborate than those of the other monks she'd seen—a rich purple that shimmered in the flickering light. Overlapping silver chevrons were stitched on its wide, draping cuffs, and the same design was banded around its broad hem.

182

The monk turned to look up at the burning hillside. Em gasped.

The back of his robe was embroidered with a black peryton.

FIFTY-TWO

The magnificently dressed stranger seemed to walk through the ring of fire burning around Em and the hellhound. Em was losing all feeling in her own shoulders, as the hellhound's massive paws pressed deeper into her skin. She could barely detect any movement from the beast at all since this monk had appeared.

The figure seemed to be issuing some kind of wordless instructions to the first monk, who made a sorry picture in his tattered long johns and burnt sackcloth cassock. Then the purple-clad stranger raised his hands. Powerful jets of water suddenly shot from the silver chevrons lining his sleeves, straight at the burning branches and the ground fires. In a matter of minutes, he had extinguished all the flames, leaving the stretch of hillside a smouldering wasteland.

Trying hard to ignore her pain and her predicament, Em stared in awe. Then she saw it. The telltale glow of an animation, a thin pulse of light running around the stranger's sleeves. Was this man the one that her mother believed was trying to steal the bone quill and *The Book of Beasts*? The one they had travelled through time to stop? If so, Em thought, gagging and coughing in the thick smoke that was choking the hillside, it looked as if they were too late.

She didn't notice him kneeling next to her until

he was already there, his hand on her cheek, his eyes burning from beneath his hood. The hound's snapping jaws were moving again, forcing her to keep still.

The monk touched her shoulder, using his sleeve to mop at the bloody cut from the hellhound's claws. Em sensed a disturbing mixture of emotions: anger, tenderness, sadness, jealousy, and something powerful that she couldn't name. It was like the feeling she got after she and Matt had a fight, a sense that she wasn't sorry but felt badly that they had fought.

The monk wiped some of the sooty filth from Em's forehead. Then he stood, pulled a drawing from the sleeve of his robes and tore it up. The hound erupted in a blaze of yellow, leaving her covered in fiery embers of light and black ash.

The monk snapped his fingers, and Em descended quickly into darkness.

FIFTY-THREE

At the very moment that Matt, Em, Simon and Sandie were fleeing across the hillside, Solon was sprinting up the tower stairs to the Abbot's study and discovering the Abbot unconscious on the floor of his ransacked cell.

The beautiful tapestry was in shreds, as if someone had deliberately cut it into pieces, and the furniture in the room—the desk, the high-backed chair, a cushioned bench where the Abbot often read for hours on end—had all been overturned and torn apart. The Abbot's desk had been upended, but Solon spotted a corner of parchment caught beneath it. He set the desk upright and was startled to find the first page of *The Book of Beasts*. How had it got here? He slid the page safely under his tunic just as he heard footsteps on the parapet below.

Solon dashed to the window. There was no sign of anyone on the parapet. But down in the cobbled courtyard, he saw two monks curled next to a tree in the middle of the compound. There were two more lolling against the portcullis, and the villagers manning the ramparts slumped over the side.

Leaning over the Abbot's body, Solon smelled the distinctive perfume of lavender, the sharp odour of hops and the sweet scent of valerian root. The rebels had taken over the monastery by putting everyone to sleep. It was a bold plan. Sleeping monks could not animate.

186

Solon hoped that wherever the Abbot had hidden the rest of the unfinished manuscript of *The Book of Beasts*, it was still safe.

Standing in the centre of the chaos, he was at a loss about what to do next.

When the Abbot had returned from his discovery of poor Brother Cornelius's body, Solon had taken the strange woman and her daughter outside and urged them to flee to safety. He decided now that his next task was to protect his old master. And then what?

Who could he trust?

You can trust me.

Solon started at the sudden voice in his head.

Carik?

Who else would it be? Brother Cornelius locked me in this cell after treating my wounds and then he left. What is happening out there?

An uprising.

Why?

Solon found the answer coming unbidden to his mind. *I think rebels wish to divert the mission of the monastery and free the beasts of Hollow Earth.*

Release me from this cell, and I can help you.

Solon's head was a muddle of mixed emotions. He had made a choice when he carried Carik back here to the monastery from Skinner's Bog. They had forged a bond, out there in the swamp, speaking to each other in their heads and fighting the Grendel together.

But could he truly trust Carik to help him?

After all, she had come to the island with the monks' enemies in the first place.

A feral howl fractured the night. Solon darted to the tower window that looked over Era Mina. He

187

could see the campfires of the stonemasons next to the foundations of his master's half-built tower. Then, from the corner of his eye, he saw a figure on the parapet. He ran to the arrow slit directly overlooking the ramparts.

Brother Thomas stood beside the parapet, a quill and parchment in his hands and a crossbow slung across his back. As Solon watched, the hellhound gargoyles that crouched silently on the turrets stretched out of their horrible stillness, became the size of bears, leaped out of the stone and galloped with eyes blazing and coats afire up the hillside after the strangers from a distant place. Their howls shook the air as they went.

Another monk appeared out of the shadows. This monk was of medium height, but stronger and more powerful than Brother Thomas in every way. Brother Thomas handed his sketch of the hellhounds to the more powerful man, who slipped it inside his richly decorated robe. The garment looked familiar to Solon but he couldn't place it at first.

Brother Thomas began to draw again. Solon had never seen a monk so purposefully and yet so mindlessly animate his art. What Brother Thomas was doing went against every vow he had taken as a member of the Order of Era Mina.

Was the monk in the regal robe controlling Brother Thomas in some way?

Solon shifted closer to the arrow slit and saw the image of a black peryton stitched on the back of the stranger's robes. At that moment, Solon remembered two important things: where he'd seen the images on the richly embroidered robe before, and how much he needed Carik's help after all.

FIFTY-FOUR

Solon and Carik crawled out of the tall window of the cell where Brother Cornelius had put her. They both tumbled to the soft, muddy ground.

Solon froze as two monks raced into view, the hems of their cassocks brushing close by his face. He pulled Carik close.

Rebels.

How do you know, Solon?

They are awake.

'Have you seen Solon, Brother Devlin?' shouted one.

'Nowhere. Cornelius never expected him to return from Skinner's Bog, curse him. We must find him and put him to sleep. Brother Thomas says we cannot succeed in our endeavour otherwise.'

When the two monks had gone, Solon grabbed Carik's hand and pulled her to her feet as gently as he could, though she still winced with pain. They sprinted into the forest, under a canopy of trees. On the cusp of the hill, smoke was shading the darkness like strokes of white paint on a black canvas.

'Are you alright?' Solon asked.

'I'm fine,' she said, rolling her stiff shoulder. 'Do you have a plan?'

'No,' Solon admitted. 'But we must find a way to stop Brother Thomas. I saw him chase after

189

the strangers as I left the Abbot's tower. He had a crossbow.'

Tell me again about these strangers.

They fell naturally into speaking in thoughts as they walked deeper into the woods. It was safer.

They have mystic qualities like ours but stronger, like no others I have encountered.

As they crested the hill, the air grew more choked with smoke and flames, but Solon knew they must go on. Through the smoke, he saw the monk in the purple robes kneeling beside the time-travelling girl, who was pinned beneath the paws of a huge two-headed black hound. Brother Thomas stood to one side, his cassock burned and filthy.

Solon touched Carik's shoulder, directing her to an opening in the briars that tangled round the trees. She steadied herself against him. They faced each other for a beat, the air crackling between them. Then, without warning, water drenched them from the tree tops.

They threw themselves into nearby bushes, shaken and afraid. Below them, the purple-cloaked monk was moving in a circle, spraying the fiery trees with water. Solon shifted over in the scratchy brambles to give Carik a better view through the undergrowth and haze.

We have to save the girl.

Why?

It was a practical question. In Carik's and Solon's world you looked after yourself first. You did not attach yourself to others outside your clan or your tribe without great trepidation. And you never risked more than you had to gain.

Solon did his best to explain.

She's one of us, Carik. We may need her help as

much as she needs ours.

Then draw something to get her out of this!

But it was hopeless; Solon had nothing to draw with. He was about to admit as much when his attention was caught by something high up near the peak of Auchinmurn.

A pulsing mass of light.

FIFTY-FIVE

The Abbey
Present Day

Matt decided not to wait until morning.

Jeannie had forced him to bin his medieval clothes, arguing that they didn't need to bring the plague back to present-day Auchinmurn. Simon's had gone, too. Matt rummaged through his laundry basket until he found the old T-Rex concert T-shirt that had belonged to his dad.

He pulled on a clean pair of jeans and dug under his bed for his boots. Then he filled his rucksack with the map of the catacombs, a box of charcoal crayons, a pad of paper, a flashlight and the wedding picture of his parents. As an afterthought, he added all the coins from his change jar. Who knew what the shiny things might buy?

Quietly closing his door behind him, he kept close to the wall in the hallway to avoid the places he knew had creaky floorboards. Then he slipped down the far stairs and into the kitchen.

Embers were spitting and crackling in the fire. Through the French doors out to the garden, Matt could see the protective shield oozing and twisting through the stone wall like candyfloss. He lifted an apple, an orange and two bananas from the fruit bowl at the centre of the kitchen table, and a bag of cereal minus its box from the pantry. Finally, after fetching his parka from the utility room, he slid the little painting of the Abbey from underneath the kitchen tablemat, where he had placed it earlier in the day.

Can't forget you, thought Matt, rolling the picture tightly and slipping it into the inside breast pocket of his parka.

The fastest way to get to Renard's study and the vault was to cut outside, across the front of the Abbey and back inside via the west tower's front door. But Matt didn't have keys to any of the outside doors. Instead he sneaked past the library, the downstairs bathroom and Simon's office until he came to the hallway that led to the gym and the swimming pool.

Matt stopped. He thought he'd heard someone coughing. He waited for a few beats. Nothing.

Digging in his back pocket, he unfolded the drawing of the Abbey's catacombs. When he and Simon had been in the Middle Ages, Matt remembered that the Abbot's tower stood on the present-day site of the swimming pool. If he could find the access to the subterranean parts of the pool, he could find the original tunnels and simply walk under the compound to the vault's outer wall. He'd think of a way inside when he got there.

He quietly opened the door to the gym, then stopped and listened again, reassuring himself that he was not being followed. Simon was sedated, Zach would not have heard any of his movements, and Renard slept in the top room of the tower above the vault and would hear nothing through the thick stone.

He headed for the pool boiler room. It was locked.

Concentrating, Matt tore a corner from his notepad and drew the doors to the room, adding a hole directly above the handle and the lock. As he put the last stroke to his shading, the doors in front of him shimmered violently, bursting into light. When they dimmed, Matt put his hand through the hole he had animated, flipping the lock from the inside.

The cramped room was dominated by a water pump, a stack of empty buckets and a long, snaking hose attached to the wall. Matt tore up his drawing, and the doors returned to normal in a flash of blue light. He was now locked inside.

He marked out the place in the middle of the floor that he hoped would take him down to the catacombs. Wiping sweat from his face, he drew a circle in charcoal with an X at its centre.

What could he animate to break open the floor? He could simply draw a hole the way he had with the door, but he wasn't sure how he could draw the dimensions of a hole deep enough to climb through.

Em would know what to draw, he thought.

A sudden banging on the door made him jump. His phone beeped a text message. Zach.

I know you're in there. Why?

Matt quickly texted back.

Need 2 help Em.

Let me come. Want 2 help her 2.

Can't take u. Not strong enough to

194

take 3 of us back.

What?? Who's in there with u?

Matt suddenly knew what to draw to get through to the tunnels underneath.

Ignoring the question in Zach's final message, he cleared the buckets and pool chemicals away from the centre of the floor. Then he wrapped the loose end of the hose around his waist, giving it a tug to make sure it felt secure. Taking out his sketchpad, he copied the room exactly as it was. When he finished, he concentrated again and began to erase the centre of the floor. It began crumbling into flecks of white and grey dust as the cement disintegrated. Scrambling to grab his backpack, Matt slipped feet first into the gaping hole he'd created, falling like Alice into a dusty darkness.

The hose around his waist stretched taut, then snapped. The impact of hitting the cold, hard ground winded Matt badly. Gasping, he pulled his knees to his chest and tried to get his breath back. Checking over his limbs, he decided he hadn't broken anything. Untying the broken hose from around his waist, he hooked his backpack over his shoulders and flipped on his torch. His phone beeped weakly.

Sorry, u can kill me later. Going to get Renard.

FIFTY-SIX

'That's okay, Zach,' said Matt aloud to himself. 'You do what you need to do.'

He pulled himself off the ground. A sharp pain stabbed through his chest. Em would have created a mattress for them to land on. Maybe he had broken a rib after all.

He was standing in a small cavern, and he could smell the sea, a briny damp that had coated the walls with a greenish-grey slime. He raised the torch, expecting to see the opening to the passage that ran underneath Renard's tower and up against the outside of the vault. Instead, the beam hit a stone wall.

Matt thumped the wall with the side of his fist, listening to the echo of his thump. Solid. Turning in a circle, he spent the next ten minutes thumping his way around the cavern. His pulse began to quicken. For the first time since he'd rolled out of bed, he began to doubt his plan.

Pressing a button on his phone, he switched the screen to a compass. The sea was to the west of the Abbey, which meant that Renard's tower was to his east. The needle on the compass shifted for a few seconds, then settled at true north. Matt stared at the wall to his right. It had to be the one he wanted.

And then he saw it. The two stones close to the curve of the cavern ceiling had no moss, no slime, nothing green on them whatsoever. They were recent additions to the chamber.

Matt quickly sketched a ladder, watching it crawl up the wall like a wooden caterpillar. He climbed to the top rung, and thumped the two dry stones. The wall beneath him began to shift and shake, leaving a gap about two metres wide beneath him. He scrambled down again, tearing up the sketch when he hit the ground, and the ladder exploded, rung by rung.

Clutching his rucksack, Matt squeezed through the gap. Midway, he felt the wall closing again, against his body. In seconds, he'd be crushed.

He realized he couldn't move forwards or backwards. He was stuck. A sharp edge of stone was digging into his injured arm. The pain brought tears to his eyes, the wall pressing hard against his chest. With one huge burst of energy, Matt squeezed himself all the way through, seconds before the stone passage sealed itself behind him with a thud. Too late, he remembered he'd left his torch on the other side.

Matt was enveloped in darkness, his only light the green digits on the face of his watch and the screen on his phone. A noise like the scampering of a hundred tiny claws stopped him in his tracks. He didn't like to think about it, but these tunnels were likely to be full of rats. The air smelled like rotting fish and wet animal.

Concentrating, Matt held his phone above his sketchbook with his right hand, illuminating the page. He scribbled with his left hand, drawing a skateboard helmet with a light embedded on the front. When he finished the animation, the helmet materialized in a scramble of reds and greens on Matt's lap.

Next up, something to ride on, he thought. *Why not?*

There wasn't time to draw a vehicle that was too elaborate, and he certainly didn't have room in the tunnels for anything too big. He sketched a scooter with a small motor on the back wheel, and added a light on the front in the shape of a shield. He'd no sooner coloured in the shield than the scooter unfolded itself in a swoosh of silver light.

Matt put on his helmet and stepped on to the scooter. He turned the gears on the handle and shot forward into the long, narrow tunnel that had once been part of the monastery's catacombs.

He regretted not bringing a more detailed map with him. The drawing of the catacombs wasn't proving as useful as he'd hoped. Up ahead, the tunnel turned west. If it didn't lead him to the wall of the vault, he'd turn back and rethink his plan.

Matt suddenly found himself at a dead end. Trusting his compass and his memory, he took his sketchpad from his backpack and began to draw his way into what he hoped was the art vault.

FIFTY-SEVEN

Zach understood Matt's motives. Leaving Em behind had been the final straw in a haystack full of them. But even as a developing Guardian, Zach always had a difficult time getting a clear reading on Matt. He had started to wonder if Matt was honing his Guardian abilities on himself, working to mask his feelings from others. At sixteen, the twins would be assigned their own Guardians, based on a close psychic connection. If Matt kept his feelings so protected, how would any Guardian ever get close enough to develop the necessary bond?

Zach was breathing hard when he reached Renard's room, where light was spilling out from under the door. He knocked and burst in, signing at warp speed.

'Matt's going to animate something. Maybe try to get back to Em. He's locked in the boiler room by the pool.'

Renard stood up from his desk at once.

'We have to stop him,' he said, grabbing a heavy set of keys from a hook behind the door.

They made their way along the corridors as quickly as they could. Zach reached the pool first. Renard swiftly unlocked the boiler-room door and flung it wide open. The space was empty, the floor intact.

'He's gone!' Zach angrily kicked the pile of blue

199

tubing that was leaning up against the far corner.

Renard stepped into the centre of the space, his fingers held to his lips. Zach watched as the older man swayed back and forth in the centre of the room, as if he was dancing.

With a jolt, Renard opened his eyes. 'Matt has discovered the catacombs.'

Closing his eyes, Zach concentrated on Matt, trying to capture the trail of his last animation— something he'd been working on with his dad. But the concrete floor was too thick and the ancient tunnels beneath too solid. All Zach could sense was the wispy image of Matt, which dissolved from his mind almost immediately.

When Zach opened his eyes, Renard was gone.

FIFTY-EIGHT

Hauling himself out of the trapdoor he'd animated into the vault, Matt was instantly overwhelmed with wonder. The joy and pleasure radiating from the art in the vault was like a thousand Christmas mornings at once.

The walls were covered in a dozen or more paintings and other kinds of art. Sculptures also filled the rough, square room, tucked into niches around the walls. Matt kicked the trapdoor shut and tore up his drawing. The animation soaked away like a puddle of coloured water.

He tore up the sketch of his helmet, leaving the only illumination in the room coming from the art itself. Each item appeared to be floating on a pillow of white light. The aura surrounding each object was like the protective shield around the Abbey walls.

The painting directly above the dissolving trapdoor was one of Turner's early oils of a burning ship on the Thames. The orange glow at the centre of the canvas was pulsing. It didn't surprise Matt to see Turner in here. If Van Gogh was an Animare, he knew it was likely that many other famous artists were, too. Next to the Turner hung a Henri Matisse, its cut-outs and thick lines almost three-dimensional. Matt was mesmerized. The pleasure was like nothing he'd ever experienced before. He had to tear himself away from its reach.

One of the niche statues was massive and egg-shaped, with a hole carved out of the top of it. In the next niche was another modern statue of an Egyptian princess with no face, just smooth white marble where her eyes and nose should have been. Standing in the niche closest to Matt was a black marble statue of an elongated figure reclining on a matching marble sepulchre, as if the figure were dead but had chosen to remain outside its tomb.

The statue opposite the reclining figure was another sort of creature altogether: a demonic-looking faun cast in bronze. The snub-nosed statue rested on muscular goat haunches, playing reed pipes with a snarl twisting its lips. Sharp, scaly horns stuck through its furrowed forehead. The gold shimmer enveloping it had a dull edge, as if its Animare aura had been smudged.

The overwhelming sense of joy Matt had felt when first entering the vault had been replaced by a thin painful pulse beating in his temples. He stepped closer to the statue, closed his eyes and concentrated. He could hear someone screaming. It seemed that the faun's sculptor had not chosen to be bound.

The near silence in the vault was suddenly shattered. Someone had summoned the security lift. Matt dashed to the tempered carbon alloy doors of the vault. Pressing his ear to the cold steel, he heard the lift grinding into action.

He had no more time to waste.

Doing his best not to let himself be distracted by the energies flowing from the art all around him, he hunted for the Duncan Fox painting his mother had copied when she had bound his father: *The Demon Within*. When he couldn't find it, he started

202

to panic.

The lift shifted gears. It was on its way back down, and Matt knew it would bring his grandpa and Zach with it. If he was going to save Em and his mum, he had to find the painting.

Fast.

He began the circuit of the vault again. When he was close to the bronze faun, he heard the elevator slow, as various security tests were implemented. Finally, when he was almost ready to give up and face his grandpa's wrath, Matt spotted it.

It was the size of a school notebook, hanging between a Constable painting of the English countryside and a painting of Robert the Bruce about to attack King Edward I's English army. The illumination from these two pictures was so dazzling that Matt wasn't surprised he had missed the small canvas tucked in the space between them.

The emergency lights in the vault began to flash. His grandpa was disarming the final security measure. Matt had run out of time.

FIFTY-NINE

When Zach realized he was alone, he ran to the sliding glass doors that opened from the pool to the lawn. Renard was jogging stiffly towards the patio and the kitchen doors. He followed at a sprint, catching up as Renard reached the patio.

As Renard unlocked the French doors, the security alarm screamed, and the emergency lights inside and outside the house began to flash.

'No!' Renard moved as fast as he could to the keypad on the utility-room wall, quickly disarming the alarm.

As Zach and Renard headed to the main foyer, their progress was halted by Jeannie in her flannel nightgown standing at the bottom of the stairs, hair in curlers and hands on her hips.

'False alarm,' said Renard, without stopping.

'Doesn't look like it from where I'm standing,' Jeannie replied. 'Where's the fire?'

Not a word, Zach!

The force of Renard's booming voice in Zach's mind startled him. He had never heard anyone other than Em in his mind before.

'What's yer hurry?' asked Jeannie, grabbing Zach's arm.

'Couldn't sleep,' signed Zach, improvising. 'Grandpa has a . . . a book for me.'

'A book?' Jeannie looked even more disbelieving. 'That's why ye got yerself dressed and came charging in through the kitchen doors? Were you thinking the book might be outside on the grass?'

Zach shrugged. It had been a long day. He had nothing else.

'Gone away wi' ye then,' said Jeannie, letting go of Zach's arm. 'And tell Mr R not to keep you up all night.'

Zach sprinted down the hall and up the stairs into Renard's tower, just in time to see him turn the secret lever on the mantel. The wall opened and revealed the steel doors of the lift.

'Matt's in the vault. But I need you to stay here, Zach. I can handle him alone,' said Renard shortly.

'How do you know that's where he's gone?'

'It's the only place that makes sense.' Renard stepped inside the lift. 'Matt must have found the old drawings of the catacombs. If I'm correct, the pool's boiler room is directly above one of the old tunnels that leads to the vault.'

Before Renard had finished punching the first code into the keypad, Zach lunged between the closing doors. They hissed shut before Renard could push him out again.

'Zach! I told you—'

'I'm sorry, Renard,' signed Zach. 'I have to come.'

As the lift began to move, the old man's anxiety felt like a low-pitched hum in Zach's mind.

'I heard you speak in my mind,' he signed.

'I hoped you would,' Renard replied with a sigh. 'Since you've been hearing Em for a couple of months, I thought that you might be able to hear me, too . . . eventually.'

The lift stopped. Renard disengaged the final

security level, pressing his palm on the pad in the control panel. The lift began its descent again. Strobe lights flashed, creating the illusion that they were travelling forwards and down. Their speed had picked up, too. If he hadn't been so anxious about Matt, Zach would have appreciated the ride more.

'Why has Matt gone to the vault?' he signed. His stomach was somersaulting, and he could feel his ears popping.

'Because,' said Renard, 'he's going to unbind his father.'

SIXTY

Renard heard the music first as the doors opened with a hiss. A soft, sultry melody.

The vault was illuminated by an eerie, animated glow. The music was much louder with the doors open. Zach shifted closer to Renard, aware of the music's increased vibrations.

'Go back up to my study—' Renard was unable to finish his sentence as the music increased to a hundred decibels. His face contorted in pain, his hands covering his ears.

'What's wrong?' Zach's heart was hammering in his chest from the intensity of the vibrations. The entire lift was shuddering.

Renard dropped to one knee in agony as the song became a thousand sharp fingernails on a chalkboard. The excruciating screech was having little effect on Zach.

Keeping his hands pressed to his ears, Renard looked at Zach desperately. 'Go!'

The lift stopped vibrating as silence fell. Ignoring Renard's plea, Zach stepped into the vault.

No, Zach! Get back inside.

Renard lunged at Zach and yanked him back, seconds before a bronze creature like a demented Pan leaped on its hind legs in front of the lift.

Zach stared in horror at the goat-man bounding back and forth on hairy legs, horns twitching from wet, fleshy cavities in its forehead. It cocked its head and scratched a cloven hoof across the stone. Then it lifted its reed pipes and began to play again.

The debilitating screech forced Renard back into the corner of the lift. The sound waves were crashing over Zach with so much force that his head was beginning to hurt.

'Is Matt doing this?'

Renard nodded, hands to his ears. 'He needs to keep us out of the vault until he's finished what he came down here to do.'

The creature continued its strange bouncing from hoof to hoof, its hairy tail waving to the music like a demented baton. The sound waves from its pipes were so forceful they were shaking the lift on its cables. Then suddenly, there was only silence and puffs of gold glitter swirling in the light from the paintings.

Renard dashed to the far side of the vault. Zach followed. Without warning, a prickly sensation at the back of his neck sent odd shivers down his spine. It wasn't pain as such, more like a brain freeze from eating an ice lolly too fast. His eyes began to water, and his fingers and toes were tingling.

'It's the power from the paintings,' said Renard, catching Zach's expression. 'Every Guardian feels a wee bit odd when he's in the presence of bound artists. I've always thought it's to make sure we remember what's been done to these men and women, and keeps us from taking the decision to bind anyone lightly.'

His face was pale as he slid to the floor under the Turner and rested his head in his hands. His grief hit Zach like a punch.

'I'm afraid Matt's gone,' Renard said. He indicated the little space between two paintings with a trembling hand—the space that had held Sandie's copy of *The Demon Within*. 'And he's taken Malcolm with him.'

SIXTY-ONE

As soon as Matt climbed out of the hole he had animated into the Abbey courtyard and stood up, he could feel the hellhound gargoyles on the ramparts straining against their moorings beneath the security spotlights. Looking up, he saw one stretch its entire body out from its parapet, floating over the darkness. Could it sense what he'd done?

Matt exhaled, forcing his mind to settle. The hellhound hunkered back into its place.

Not for the first time that night, he wished Em was with him.

Ducking under the shadows of the arch that led through Jeannie's garden and down to the jetty, he tore up his sketches of the statue and his last tunnel.

'Sorry, Grandpa,' he mumbled. 'You too, Zach.'

So far, he felt as if he'd done everything holding his breath, afraid he'd make a mistake and lose his chance.

The wind had picked up, bringing squalls of rain across the bay. Matt fastened his parka and pulled on a black hat. He shoved his hands in his pockets, finding a pair of fingerless gloves and pulling them on.

You're stalling, Matt Calder, he thought to himself.

The next part of his plan was the part that scared him most of all. Stealing the painting from the vault

210

had been easy. He had known what to expect and done his research in preparation. To unbind his dad from a painting was another task all together.

To bind someone in a painting called for the combined powers of both Animare and Guardian. It was a safe guess to assume that both were needed to achieve the reverse as well. Matt was starting to doubt he was powerful enough to pull it off on his own.

Stop dwelling on failure. You're better and stronger than that, he thought.

He could feel the intensity of the painting throbbing against his back, where it was tucked inside his rucksack. He would succeed. He'd free his dad, and together they would rescue Sandie and Em. Then they could be a family again.

A family.

Pulling the rucksack tighter on his shoulders, Matt jogged down towards the bay.

At the end of the jetty, he unknotted the tether on the Abbey's rowing boat, climbed aboard and pushed it away from the dock. He pulled his sketchpad from his front pocket. Closing his eyes for a second, concentrating on the lines and the shading of his drawing, he let his imagination and his fingers take over.

A lantern flared into life on the prow of the boat. Grabbing the oars from under the seat, Matt shoved them one at a time through the rowlocks and began to row towards the smaller island of Era Mina.

*   *   *

From the long tower window, Renard lifted his

binoculars, scanning the lawn, the stables, the pool wing and the jetty, and then out across the bay. Zach was doing the same from the front windows, scanning the edge of the thick woods that created a natural barrier between the Abbey and the main road around the island. There was no sign of Matt anywhere.

Renard tapped Zach on the shoulder. 'Did you lock up the rowing boat after you and the twins last used it?'

'I think so,' replied Zach cautiously. He wasn't sure he had remembered to lock up the boat at all.

Renard looked out at the bay again. The moon was hidden behind a bank of heavy clouds spitting rain on the island and fogging up the tower windows. The bay was a band of black water, with only the distant lights on the islands of Arran and Bute giving the scene any perspective.

'Go and activate the lighthouse on Era Mina, Zach,' said Renard. 'The switch is in the boathouse. If Matt's taken to the water, we can use the light to try to track him.'

As Zach darted from the room, Renard kept scanning the water, back and forth, concentrating on any change in the waves and shifts in the moonlit shadows.

Where are you, Matt? he thought. *Where are you?*

Then Renard saw it—a glowing silver thread of light floating ethereally across the water.

'Got you,' he said, dropping his binoculars to his chest in relief. 'You can't hide an animation from me, son.'

*   *   *

Matt was having a difficult time keeping on course, what with the wind, the rain and the building anxiety about what he was about to do. He was under no illusion that his grandfather would be tracking him. But if his plan worked, he'd be back in the Middle Ages before Renard discovered where he had gone.

Matt tore up the sketch of the lantern, shoving the pieces into his pocket with the other scraps. As the boat hit ground, he jumped out and dragged it up on to the rocky beach, stabbing its iron anchor into the sand. Then he dodged as fast as he could across the wet rocks, concentrating on his footing.

He was counting on the fact that he couldn't hide an animation from his grandfather.

SIXTY-TWO

The kitchen was buzzing with activity when Renard ran in to grab his raincoat and boots, despite it being three o'clock in the morning. Jeannie hadn't returned to bed. A roaring fire was blazing in the hearth, the kettle was whistling, Jeannie was making toast, and Zach was buttering it with a mug of hot chocolate topped with melting marshmallows set in front of him. A swoosh of light from the Era Mina lighthouse was beaming across the lawn every three minutes.

Simon suddenly marched into the kitchen, dressed in his rain gear.

'What are you doing out of bed?' Renard asked with surprise.

'You need me,' Simon answered. His eyes were still heavy with sleep, the cut above his eye a rainbow of blues, pinks and yellows. He held his arm stiffly.

'Matt's gone to Era Mina with *The Demon Within*,' said Renard. 'He's going to try and unbind his father.'

'I know,' said Simon. 'I felt the whole thing. Let's go.'

Zach started up from the table.

Renard shook his head firmly. 'No, Zach. Not this time.'

'Malcolm is dangerous,' Simon told his son. 'Very dangerous. And if Matt manages to unbind him, Malcolm will not only be dangerous but unstable.'

'Because he's been bound for so long?' prompted Zach.

Renard fastened his coat and headed to the French doors. 'Because no one has ever been unbound and survived,' he said.

'Matt doesn't know that!' Zach signed, aghast. 'We need to stop him.'

'And we will,' said Simon. 'But you need to leave it to us.'

Jeannie walked with Simon and Renard to the doors, talking to them as she went. They had their backs to Zach, making it impossible for him to read their lips. He felt a rush of anger. They had turned away from him on purpose.

*   *   *

Matt lurked in the darkness until he saw Simon and Renard unlock the boathouse, pull the cover from the speedboat and shoot out into the bay towards Era Mina, with Simon behind the wheel.

Matt climbed on a jet ski he'd animated in advance, copying the design he and Em had drawn to rescue Zach in 1871. With the speedboat's engine masking the jet ski's roar, Matt cut through the darkness, keeping well away from Simon and Renard, back towards Auchinmurn.

He almost blew his whole plan when he crashed the jet ski on to the Auchinmurn shore faster and harder than he intended, the momentum propelling him across the boulders shored up against the tide and planting him face-down on the rocks. He lay in the cold and wet for a minute or

215

two, suddenly feeling sorry for himself. He didn't want to do this alone any more. He was not good alone. He needed Em. He needed someone— anyone. He needed his dad.

Climbing back on to his feet, Matt wiped the tears and the rain from his eyes and set off into the interior of the island.

*   *   *

Zach paced in front of the kitchen fire, his adrenalin spiking from a combination of caffeine, sugar and a large dose of irritation. Why did the adults have to treat him like such a child? He was as capable as they were, maybe more, of talking Matt out of this. They should at least have given him a chance.

He closed his eyes and stilled his breathing. It was always difficult to track Matt in his mind, but he gave it his best shot. Concentrating hard, he thought he could feel a flash of grief and emotion. Then the image of a putrid swamp glimmered through.

Zach snapped his eyes open. Matt wasn't on Era Mina.

Sprinting into the utility room, he grabbed his parka, falling over himself as he tried to pull on his boots while hopping to the French doors.

'Wait just one wee minute!' said Jeannie, blocking his way. 'Where do you think yer going?'

'I know where he is!' Zach signed, dropping his left boot. 'By the time my dad and Renard figure out that Matt's tricked them, it'll be too late. Jeannie, I'm the best possible person to talk Matt out of this. Let me go!'

216

He put his hand on Jeannie's forearm and held her gaze, concentrating, drawing her distress and her determination from her, absorbing her feelings in his own psyche the way he had been learning from his dad. When he believed he had inspirited her enough to make his escape, he lifted his hand away.

He had hardly taken two steps when Jeannie's hand shot out and grabbed him again.

'I'm chuffed that ye thought you could persuade me with your abilities, but you forget I've been running this place since yer dad was a wean, and you're still not going anywhere.'

Zach slumped on to the couch, angry and frustrated, and watched Jeannie answer the phone. When she hung up, she lifted her own coat from its peg and her orange safety vest, pulled on her boots and waved Zach to the door.

'That was your dad,' said Jeannie. 'You were right. Matt tricked them and he seems to have done something to the petrol tank on the boat. They're stuck on Era Mina. I'm taking the small fishing boat over wi' some petrol and you've to go find Matt.' She leaned close to Zach. 'Yer dad says under no circumstances are you to do anything other than try to stop him from unbinding his dad. Promise?'

Nodding emphatically, Zach pulled open the French doors.

Jeannie put her hand on Zach's shoulder. 'We need to know where Matt is,' she said gently.

Zach looked at Jeannie. 'He's gone to Skinner's Bog.'

SIXTY-THREE

The rain was making progress difficult. Every three or four steps Matt made, he'd slip back another two or three. When the climb became so steep that he was going backwards more than forwards, he got on his hands and knees and battled onwards on all fours. He felt acutely grateful for the head torch that he had animated.

Skinner's Bog was high within the densest part of the forest, almost at the pinnacle of Auchinmurn Isle. Matt, Em and Zach had explored the site exhaustively over the summer, while avoiding the small patch of bog that still existed. The swamp was hidden behind the ruins of a megalith of standing stones called the Devil's Dyke, a couple of which still remained upright.

When Matt reached the stones, he ducked behind the upright stones, pulling his binoculars from under his parka and checking to be sure he was not being followed. He had a faint, rainy view of Era Mina and the old pencil tower across the moonlit water, together with the northern side of the Abbey.

Matt moved nimbly across the planks of wood that he and Zach had put down in the summer as a makeshift bridge over the swampy ground, ducking into the opening of the only cave left exposed on the hillside. A small stone bench sat under the canopy of the rock, cut from the cave wall by one of

Matt's ancestors to enjoy the breathtaking views.

The rain had finally stopped, but the wind was blowing at gale force. Matt checked his watch. It would be daylight soon. He needed to do this while he was still under the cover of darkness.

He pulled his sketchpad and a metal biscuit tin layered with skateboard and gamer stickers from his backpack, double-checking that the painting was still secure in his pack's inside pocket. A glimmer of yellow light spilled from the flap of the pocket.

'Soon, Dad. Promise,' Matt whispered.

Popping open the top of the tin, he lifted out his charcoals. Then he took the rolled-up picture from the pocket of his parka, remembering Duncan Fox's words:

I myself have used the tapestry to make several painting trips. Only the other day, I found myself in an awkward situation with one of our mutual ancestors.'

Fox had made this painting on one of his medieval trips, unwittingly providing Matt with a new way into the past.

Animating through a painting was not an exact science. He worked out that this painting had actually been created a little lower down the hill. Matt hoped he wasn't about to confront Duncan Fox as he was painting it.

Matt's plan was to animate through the top left section of the painting, where Fox had captured the standing stones and the Devil's Dyke in brilliant hues of brown and green. Concentrating on the bold brush strokes and sweeping lines, Matt used a blue charcoal crayon to animate the scene. He hoped he could draw on the island's own mystical

219

resonance at this sacred spot, near these standing stones, to amplify and boost the animation.

As soon as his fingers touched the page, a white light flooded his imagination, flaring to brilliance when he shaded the peak of the tallest standing stone.

SIXTY-FOUR

Skinner's Bog
Auchinmurn Isle
Middle Ages

Matt shot on to the Scottish hillside in an explosion of light shavings and gold dust, as if he'd been fired from an invisible cannon. The island was shrouded in the bleak mist of early dawn, its craggy peak cloaked beneath the creeping gloom.

Unable to control his forward momentum, he hit the stony hillside hard, tumbling head first into a thick tangle of bramble bushes at the edge of the Devil's Dyke. Scrambling to his knees, Matt crawled quickly under the cover of the thicket, glancing back to the spot that was still shimmering with a pale yellow light. He counted to three before taking a moment to breathe, settle and take stock.

Simon, Renard and Zach were all Guardians, not Animare. There was no one else who would be able to follow him through time.

Wriggling through the dense undergrowth, Matt peered out at the landscape. He had landed on the perimeter of Skinner's Bog as he had hoped he would. In this time, it filled the entire space before him, a green, fetid marsh within the tight circle of standing stones. The stones were all the size of trees, not the least bit like the ruins of the present day.

221

Yanking his zip up to his chin, Matt was glad he had taken the time to dress warmly. The air was cold and damp, the fog soaking every surface around him in small drops of water.

He looked beyond the bog at the waves crashing against the rocky coastline, the monastery and its fortressed wall dominating the landscape. Beyond the wall, curling towers of smoke rose from village chimneys like grey ghosts.

Em and his mum were down there somewhere. Matt hoped they had survived the chase and had found a place to hide.

Em! Can you hear me?

Nothing.

With the rising sun came strange noises from deep within the bog, a low, guttural gurgling. It was followed by a wild, frenzied howl, like a wolf or a wild boar, then a slurping sort of swallow.

Blocking out these disturbing sounds, Matt unwrapped his mum's copy of *The Demon Within* from his rucksack. The figure of the demon pulsed with more brilliance than Matt had ever seen. It looked as if it were about to burst out of the frame on its own.

Last chance to change your mind, Matt thought to himself.

Sitting cross-legged in front of the painting, he flipped open his sketchbook. Unsure what he needed to do to unbind an Animare, he thought he'd begin by copying the demon and concentrating with all the power of his imagination so that his dad would appear and not the demon itself.

Matt began to sketch, slowly at first, outlining precisely the lines of Fox's drawing and letting the horrible demon enter his imagination and form

222

itself, large and scaly, in the palette of his mind. Red, blue, yellow, copper and brown, curved lines, pulsing circles and sharp angles exploded in Matt's brain. His eyes ached as if they were burning into the back of his head. He squeezed them closed.

Something deep inside Matt's brain was calling to him, a distant voice telling him that he must keep the actual demon from animating or all would be lost. The demon was pushing against his temples. He felt its claws ripping at his flesh, trying to escape from his imagination. He had to hold it in place.

Matt was hurting. His head felt like it was about to burst.

Then he lost control of his fingers. They were skating across the page, driven by the beast within him. Matt's eyes were on fire. The voice grew more insistent.

A minute more. A minute more.

The demon was dissolving into rainbows of light, each colour stabbing his mind like a laser. Matt's eyes felt ten times too big for his head. He couldn't take the pain any more. His whole being was on fire.

I'm sorry, Dad. I'm so sorry. I can't do this alone. I need Em—

Matt's eyes flew open. A torrent of white light poured from them, burning into the painting, bands of light and waves of colour expanding from the picture. Matt was thrown backwards by the force of the illumination, landing hard against one of the standing stones. The impact knocked the air from his lungs, buckling him over, gasping and choking.

Then, as if a curtain was slowly closing on his imagination, the light in Matt's head dimmed.

223

Before everything went black, an image tugged at his exhausted mind—something in the landscape when he'd appeared on the hillside. A mistake in his surroundings.

What had happened to the tower on Era Mina? When he'd scanned the landscape a few minutes ago, there had been no tower. No stonemasons laying stone, no campfires or boats carrying supplies back and forth. Not as it had been when he had left Em and his mother on that hillside.

Matt was too exhausted to move or to think clearly. But one thought hung in his head, as clear as a bell.

He had arrived too soon.

Then he passed out.

PART FOUR

SIXTY-FIVE

Skinner's Bog
Auchinmurn Isle
Middle Ages

Malcolm Calder loomed over an unconscious Matt, taking a moment to process that this boy was his son. With no memory of his time locked in the painting, his body and spirit having been in a kind of pause mode, Malcolm's mind was resetting like a video game. As he took in his surroundings, his consciousness was slowly reforming the same set of opinions, biases, ambitions and festering resentments that he had held before he had been bound.

Malcolm looked down at his shirt and his jeans. They were paint-splattered and covered in grime. Then he held his hands out in front of his face, flexing and cracking his stiff knuckles, stretching his back, twisting his head back and forth, loosening his neck muscles. Lifting his fingers to his face, he tentatively touched his cheek, feeling a furrow of unfinished flesh scoring across his eye and skating down through his cheekbone. His cheek was soft and spongy to his touch. When Malcolm stared at his fingers, they were covered in a red, gummy substance, like a melted crayon. He felt no pain— just an odd tingling sensation behind his empty eye socket.

227

He absorbed every detail of Matt's face, amazed at how grown-up he looked. So he had been bound . . . for how long? Ten years? Anger caught him around the throat. Ten years of his life, gone. All his plans frozen in time, like him. Sandie and his father would pay for what they'd done.

The boy looked a lot like he had at that age. Malcolm wondered if Em took more after her mother. He scanned the hillside. Was she here?

The sun was rising. Down to his left he recognized the Abbey, its towers and high stone wall—and off the coast, Auchinmurn's sister island Era Mina . . . without a tower.

Without a tower?

And then every synapse fired in Malcolm's head at once. He knew where he was—*when* he was. He shook his head in disbelief.

'So you have done the impossible, Matt,' he murmured. 'You have unbound me, and you have brought me back to the time when all this began. How very exciting! I knew we had created something special when you and your sister were born.'

His son was deep in the suspended sleep of an Animare whose imagination had been stretched to the limits. He'd be out for a while. Malcolm rested his cold hand on Matt's warm chest. Summoning his weak reserves of energy, he dragged Matt as far from Skinner's Bog as he could manage. He settled the boy under the thick cover of the bracken that formed the border of the furthest part of the Devil's Dyke. Then he pressed his hand to his son's neck, feeling for his pulse. It remained healthy.

Carefully, he slid Matt's black hat from his head. If he unrolled it all the way down, it covered enough of his incomplete cheek and eye socket, until he could find something better.

'You did your best,' he whispered, brushing hair from Matt's face. 'And I can live with the flaws.' He poked his finger into the cavity where his cheek should have been, caressing the exposed bone and the sharp points of his incisor teeth. 'Besides, this incomplete visage may work to my advantage.

'I will be back for you soon, son. But for now, I can't have you wandering through the Middle Ages without me.'

Malcolm made sure that Matt's parka was fastened tightly and he was well protected from the elements. Who knew how long it might be before he could return to fetch him?

Heavy clouds sailed across the brightening sky. Malcolm rolled up the little landscape painting he guessed Matt had used to travel here, and stuck it into the waistband of his paint-splattered jeans. He couldn't risk it being destroyed. It was the only way home.

Kissing the tips of his fingers, he set the kiss on his son's lips. Then he jogged quickly into the woods and down the hillside towards the water, the Abbey's towers lit by the sun now breaking through the mist. He paused at a group of tall birch trees.

Better wait until dark, he thought. No reason to put himself at risk.

Pulling some branches over himself for cover, he curled in a nest of leaves in the middle of the tall trees. In this position, Malcolm Calder slept the sleep of the dead.

*   *   *

When the moon was rising and dusk was cloaking the islands, Malcolm started down the hillside again. At the bay, he rolled up his jeans and jogged through the shallow water, looking for a way to cross to Era Mina without calling attention to his presence.

He spotted a primitive rowing boat tied up beneath a willow tree, its hull bouncing in the choppy water, its oars under the plank seat. Knowing he was now virtually invisible in the dark, he climbed aboard, using an oar to push off.

As he rowed into the channel between the islands, Malcolm set his oars across his lap, letting the craft bob lazily in the waves. He was stunned by the brilliant display of stars in the medieval sky above. Behind him, the monastery was a shadowy outline, the noises from the monks and their animals muted and distant.

Pulling Matt's hat down over his head, Malcolm picked up the oars and headed on towards the dark side of Era Mina.

SIXTY-SIX

Three Days Later...

Solon summoned the peryton the moment he realized that the glow at the peak of Auchinmurn by Skinner's Bog was coming from a powerful animation. He and Carik had flown low to avoid any watchful eyes. Now Solon jumped from the peryton's back before the beast's hooves hit the ground at the ridge of trees on the outer edge of Skinner's Bog, close to the Devil's Dyke.

Solon found the source of the light almost immediately. It was a small painting of a demon, a scaly, red, hairless monster. Turning it over, he saw scribbles in a language that he didn't understand.

How had such an evil-looking painting arrived at this isolated spot?

'Solon,' Carik called in a low voice. 'Over here. There's a boy.'

They studied the boy and his strange bag of belongings tucked under the brambles. Was he under the same sleeping spell as the monks at the monastery?

'He's been here since today's storm at least, maybe longer,' said Carik, noting the wet leaves covering his clothing and the wind burn on the boy's cheeks. 'He's soaked.'

A bubble of fetid air hissed to the surface of the bog and floated towards them.

'We mustn't stay here,' said Solon, tucking the painting of the demon inside his shirt. 'Nor must the boy, unless he wants to be a meal for the Grendel.'

They lifted the drenched boy on to the peryton's back. Carik fetched his belongings. After puzzling over how to open the strange bag for a while, she gave up, hooked one of the straps over her shoulder and joined Solon on the peryton's back.

Solon supported the boy in front of him, the boy's arms flopping across the peryton's shimmering antlers.

'The peryton's never flown with three of us. Hold on tight,' Solon warned.

Carik wrapped her arms tightly round Solon's waist, as the peryton rose up on its hind legs, gracefully pivoting and then galloping along the hillside to the cliff. With its silver wings expanding, the beast lifted its forelegs into the air and flew up over moonlit Auchinmurn and the bay. Then it turned and swooped inland again, towards an abandoned cottage on the northern tip of the island.

'Who do you think he is?' asked Carik, her breath warm on Solon's ear.

'I don't know,' replied Solon. The peryton was carrying them across the wind as if they weighed little more than a feather. 'But I think he may have something to do with what's going on in the monastery.'

SIXTY-SEVEN

The next morning, Matt woke up to the stench of horse manure and the sensation of a sheep chewing slowly on the sleeve of his parka. He felt loose and strange.

'Hey!' he croaked.

Rolling away from the sheep, he landed directly on the offending pile of manure. He got unsteadily to his feet, straw and stalks of grass sticking to his hair. His arm was thick with muck.

He was in a stable, still in the clothes he'd been wearing when he'd sneaked down into the catacombs. The wind was chilly, howling in through the wide cracks in the stone. The odour in the hut grew even more disgusting as it mingled with the smell of the sea.

'Awake at last?'

'Where did you come from?' asked Matt groggily.

'We slept in the caves, though we did not sleep as well as you.'

Matt gawked at the speaker with her white-blonde hair wrapped loosely in a scarf and her deep blue eyes twinkling with laughter. Her smile was amazing. Matt knew he was staring, but he couldn't help himself. She was dressed in a brown shift under a loose, black, wool tunic and leggings tucked in laced sheepskin boots. One arm looked injured, and was bound with clean cloths.

233

'I have food,' she said. 'Come outside. It's a beautiful morning.'

Stepping outside, Matt was blinded by the radiant sunlight. The girl handed him an apple, which he accepted and bit into hungrily.

'I am Carik from the north.' She pointed out over the distant islands. 'Solon and I found you last night at Skinner's Bog.'

Matt was still gawking at the girl. She looked fragile, yet she addressed him with purpose and carried herself with strength. He finished the apple in three bites. It was sweet and delicious.

A tall, blond young man, his hair shaggy but shorter than Matt's, was leaning against the outside wall of the stable, watching him with narrowed eyes. Solon, presumably. He didn't look happy.

'Where am I?' Matt asked.

'You are on the island of Auchinmurn,' said Carik.

'We are hiding,' said Solon abruptly. 'The monastery has been taken over by rebels. Their leader, 'the prophet' as they're calling him, is a stranger to the islands, but somehow he is wearing the purple robes of the Order's first martyr.'

'This prophet has put a sleeping spell on all of the monks who are not on his side,' added Carik. 'We wondered if you were under the same spell.'

'The monastery's been taken over already?' said Matt, aghast. 'How long was I asleep?'

Solon and Carik both looked puzzled.

'We are not aware of how long you were asleep or even how you came to be at Skinner's Bog,' said Carik , 'but—'

'You say, "already",' Solon interrupted. 'You knew about this attack?'

In one fluid movement, he had reached behind his back, pulled a sword from his belt and thrust its tip against Matt's chest. Matt slapped the blade away, backing against a tree. Solon held his position.

Matt was beside himself. Had he missed his chance? Were his mother and Em already dead? Could you cross paths with yourself in a different time? His head was tumbling with possibilities.

He suddenly remembered the last thought he'd had before sliding into unconsciousness.

'The tower,' he said urgently. 'The one on Era Mina. Have you started building it?'

Suddenly, Matt wished he'd read more of Em's science fiction books. As soon as that thought jumped into his head, he felt a twinge in his heart. What he really wished was for Em to be here with him, to help him figure out what he should do next.

Solon was looking more and more suspicious. 'We started the tower for my master Brother Renard four days ago, the day after the Viking attack.'

Matt felt ill. Everything was flooding back. Stealing the painting, unbinding his father. He and his dad must have arrived at dawn four days ago, just after the Viking attack, and just before they started building the tower. Jeez. He'd been asleep for four days. And his dad . . . What had happened to his dad?

A terrifying thought hit him squarely between the eyes.

What if his dad was the prophet, the leader of the rebels? What if his dad was the person out of time that his mum and Duncan Fox had detected? What if his dad was the one searching for the bone quill?

What if everything that was happening was all Matt's fault?

'Brother Renard?' he said, grasping the only thing Solon had said that didn't make him feel like puking. 'My grandfather's called Renard. It means fox, I think.' Another thought struck him. 'Duncan *Fox*. Of course. Names change over time. I should have put this together before.'

Solon and Carik exchanged glances. Matt knew he was rambling.

'Have you seen this rebel leader?' he asked, trying to swallow on a sandpaper throat.

'The villagers say he is a horrible demon,' Carik answered. 'I heard them talking two days after the attack, as I made my way to this place to fetch berries for the wound I sustained in the battle.' She gestured at her bound arm.

'I heard them talking then, too, in the chapel,' said Solon. 'I have seen only glimpses of him, like tonight, on the hillside. He has been rousing rebellion and anarchy in the other monks since he arrived.'

Four days.

'You know who this man is,' Solon said, watching Matt's expression.

Matt flinched. 'Does it matter?'

'Yes. This island has secrets that must be protected. It's a dangerous place and it does not take kindly to strangers. Is he an Animare?'

Matt put his head in his hands. 'No,' he said through his fingers. 'He's a Guardian. He . . . protects Animare.'

'I don't think he was protecting Brother Thomas on the parapet last night,' said Solon. 'I think he

236

was controlling him, making him animate the hellhounds from the carvings on our ramparts. Is this possible?'

Matt nodded again. Anything was possible. He couldn't think straight.

Em! Can you hear me? Please say you can hear me?

'And you are also an Animare?' asked Solon, his tone guarded.

'My name's Matt . . . Matt Calder and I'm a hybrid,' said Matt dully. 'A freak of nature. My mum is an Animare and my dad . . . my dad is a Guardian. I have a mixture of their talents.'

'Where have you come from?' prodded Solon.

Matt suddenly felt incredibly homesick—not just for his sister, but for Zach, Simon, his grandpa, his mum and his dad. *His dad.*

'I've come from very far away.'

Solon wrinkled his nose. 'Well, you should clean yourself up. You stink of manure.'

Laughing, Carik indicated a small water trough outside the stable. Humiliation piled on top of guilt as Matt silently washed the manure from his sleeve and combed some of the stink from his hair with his fingers.

A distant bell pealed out through the still morning air.

'Lauds—morning prayers,' said Solon. 'If the rebellion has succeeded, the rebels and this prophet will be gathering in the monastery.' He swept his blond hair into a ponytail and tied it with a strip of leather. 'I need to be sure that they have not harmed Brother Renard. If they've put him to sleep, he'll be safe, but if they've taken him . . . his powers will be far too easy to control.' He touched

Carik's shoulder. 'You stay here with this boy.'

Matt bristled. He didn't like the way Solon said 'boy'.

'Wait!' he said as Solon headed into the woods. 'I'll come with you.'

'No,' said Solon without turning round. 'I don't trust you.'

'Then why are you leaving me here with her?' said Matt, his anger rising. 'I could easily take her hostage or something.'

'I am capable of protecting myself,' said Carik sharply.

'I do not want you near the monastery,' Solon said.

'I appreciate that you gave me shelter, but I don't care about what *you* want,' said Matt. 'I need to know what happened to my mum and my sister, and I've already wasted enough time. So I'm coming with you whether you like it or not.'

SIXTY-EIGHT

Solon stopped and stared.

'Your sister? The girl with the stripe in her hair was your sister?'

'Yes! Have you seen her?'

'I met her, with the Abbot. She and her— your mother came through the tapestry. Their sudden appearance was . . . a shock.'

Matt's eyes were burning with anger. 'I need to know where they are!'

His distress was drumming loudly in Solon's mind.

'I am sorry,' Solon said, hesitating.

'Sorry for what? You better not have hurt them.' Matt yanked the sword from Solon's hand and tossed it across the clearing. Then he grabbed Solon's shoulders as if he could shake the answer from him.

Solon jerked himself from Matt's grasp. The boy lunged at his back instead. Solon heard him coming, side-stepping just in time. The action only served to enrage Matt more.

'I am sorry because your sister and your mother were caught in a fire that burned up the hillside last evening,' said Solon, backing away. 'We saw the flames engulf the clearing.'

'You're lying!'

'We're not,' said Carik.

'They left the Abbot's tower to meet up with

239

others,' said Solon. 'After the Abbot discovered the bone quill was gone and poor Brother Cornelius had been butchered.'

'Your sister was trapped by one of the hellhounds,' said Carik softly. 'There was nothing we could do before the flames closed in on her.'

'You were there and you didn't help her!' screamed Matt, shoving Solon back into the trunk of a tree. 'And my mother? You—'

Solon grabbed a nearby slop pail and swung it against Matt's head to defend himself. Matt saw the swing coming but not soon enough to duck, and the rim of the bucket sliced across his forehead, cutting it.

Rage and blood blinded Matt. All the terror and shame and fury he'd been feeling exploded through his fists and his feet. He threw himself at Solon, pummelling him ferociously.

Carik tried to get between them, but she timed her interference badly. A direct kick to the back of her knees brought her down. Solon's eyes widened in fury, and he lunged at Matt, the two of them rolling across the dirt.

Carik got quickly to her feet and grabbed Matt's hair, yanking him off Solon. 'Stop!' she commanded, struggling to keep Matt's arms and fists under control with her own weakened arm.

Breathless and aching, Matt pushed Carik away. He wiped blood and tears from his eyes with his sleeve, adrenalin churning in his stomach. Then he rolled on to his side and vomited. When he sat up, guilt and heartbreak overwhelmed him.

He had been too early, and now he was too late.

Carik tore some strips from a turnip sack and dunked them into the water trough, passing Matt and Solon each two wet strips.

'Clean up your wounds,' she said angrily. Then she headed over to the pigsty, where she scooped up a handful of mud and brought the thick muck over to the boys.

Matt cleaned his face as best he could with the thin, coarse strips. When the open wound was visible above his eye, Carik slathered mud on top of it. Matt tried to pull away. She glared. He stopped.

'Be still,' she said. 'It'll dry in the sun and keep the wound closed.'

Solon packed his nostrils with leaves to staunch the bleeding, as Carik wiped mud across the slice on his cheek. 'We'll try to find out what happened to them,' he said in a low voice. 'But if they survived the hellhounds, I don't think they could possibly have survived the fire.'

After a beat, he leaned towards Matt and offered him his hand.

Matt stared at Solon's outstretched palm, his face blood-streaked and wet with tears.

'If you're going to find your father and stop this rebellion,' said Solon, 'then you're going to need our help.'

'How do you know we're talking about my father?' Matt whispered.

'Because you said that the stranger who has come to our island is a Guardian,' explained Solon, 'and you hesitated before telling us that your father is a Guardian, too. We may be peasants, but we're not stupid.'

Matt nodded, accepting Solon's hand unsteadily. 'I'm sorry I hurt you,' he mumbled. 'And thanks for the offer. But I think I need to do this on my own. After all, my dad is the only family I have left.'

SIXTY-NINE

Auchinmurn Isle
Middle Ages
The Night Before

Sandie had lost her footing while scrambling to Em's defence against the slobbering hellhound, and was tumbling head over heels back down the hillside. Even her dress snagging on bramble bushes was doing nothing to stop her freefall.

'Em!' she screamed.

In one ungainly roll through a thorny briar, Sandie slowed enough to see a woman in a modern orange safety vest running into the smoking blaze. Before disappearing behind the curtain of smoke, the woman turned and smiled at Sandie.

Sandie couldn't believe what she was seeing. How was that possible?

But then she was off again, slipping out of the briar, her head bouncing off a tree root. She lunged and caught the end of the root just as the rest of her body swung off the edge of the overhang.

Her hands were bleeding, and she had cuts across her arms and legs. Her dress was torn and filthy. Scrambling to get a better grip on the overhang, her legs bicycled against the rocks. It was a long drop to the beach. Sandie dolphin-kicked furiously, trying to heave herself up on to solid ground, but the tree root was not having it. As if

242

in slow motion, it lifted from the soil. Her arms flailing in the air, Sandie dropped off the edge.

*   *   *

The woman in the safety vest marched into the smouldering haze in time to see a monk in an ornate purple cassock crouching down to lift a sleeping Em into his arms.

'Stop right there and leave the wean alone,' Jeannie demanded, her hands on her ample hips, 'before we both do something we might regret.'

Malcolm froze at the sight of the Abbey's housekeeper standing amid the ash and debris of Em's fears. He had spent his entire life listening to Jeannie. She'd been like a mother to him, and he wished he was confronting anyone but her.

Taking a step back, he dropped his hood to reveal the grotesque skeletal shell of his face.

Jeannie didn't flinch. Her stance remained resolute, her grey hair recently shampooed and set, her short leather boots tight on her thick ankles and her best wool coat peeping out from underneath the safety vest. It was as if she'd left the house to go to church, instead of travelling through time to meet a monster.

'You don't scare me, Malcolm Calder,' she said. 'I'm taking the lass and we're going home. All I ask is ye think about what you're doing here, and let us bring you home, too. This isn't right and you know it. You'll fracture history and change everything.'

Malcolm burst out laughing. The old lady was making demands on him? On Malcolm Calder, who was destined to be so much more than a Guardian and a father? He flipped the cowl of his robe back up over his head, concealing his ruined face beneath its folds again.

'You always did see the best in all of us, didn't you, Jeannie?'

'It's still in there, son,' she said, her voice and her stance softening. 'Come home, why don't you? For the sake of your weans and your poor dad.'

'One day, Jeannie, you'll realize there's a demon in all of us,' said Malcolm. 'I'm simply choosing to let mine free.'

He turned back towards his daughter. But before he could reach down and pick her up, the peryton crashed through the tops of the trees and swooped down. With a toss of its head, it flung Em up from the leaves and on to its back and flew out over the blackened treetops, down to the beach—and out of sight.

Malcolm howled in rage. 'You cannot stop me, Jeannie! No one can! *I am unbound!* I found the bone quill and took it and I hold it here, against my heart.' He struck at a leather pouch around his neck. 'My own son released me from the purgatory into which my father and my wife had bound me.' He took a step towards Jeannie. 'I have killed, controlled, *ruled* the superstitious fools on this island and when I find *The Book of Beasts*, Hollow Earth, the world and the future will all be mine!'

Faster than Jeannie could have believed possible, he vanished into the smouldering woods, the firelight glinting on the embroidered black peryton of his robes.

Jeannie did not give chase. Instead, she kneeled

244

down and began to brush away the layer of ash covering the ground, before scrabbling at the soil with her fingers, burrowing her hands deep into the earth.

Then she closed her eyes and imagined.

SEVENTY

Sandie had landed in Simon's waiting arms with a thump.

'I've got you,' said Simon, steadying himself with a wince. 'Though to be honest, I need to put you down right now.' He set her on her feet and rubbed at his injured shoulder.

'Simon!' Sandie gasped. She spun around and stared up at the cliff. 'I thought I saw . . .'

'Jeannie?' said Simon. 'You did.'

'How did I never realize she was an Animare?'

Simon smiled. 'None of us did. It was the way that she wanted it. Renard's her Guardian, and she made him swear an oath years ago to keep her secret. Her connection to these islands runs even deeper than ours.'

The peryton suddenly swooped down and landed on the sand with a snort. Em lay draped across its back.

'Oh, Em!' Sandie rushed to her stirring, groaning daughter and lifted her from the peryton's back, covering her with kisses.

The peryton flicked its brilliant white head and leaped into the sky in a trail of shimmering light.

'Is Jeannie the one who animated the peryton?' Sandie asked, still trying to adjust to all that was happening.

'Yes.'

Sandie used the torn hem of her skirt to wipe

soot from Em's forehead. 'She looks so young . . . they are both still so young.' She glanced around. 'Did Matt get home safely?'

Simon was silent for a second. 'Matt returned to find you and Em. He's somewhere on the island, but we don't know where.'

Sandie's hands flew to her face. 'We need to find him!'

Simon knew he'd never get Sandie to return with him if he told her that Matt had come to the Middle Ages with Malcolm. They needed to return to Renard and the Abbey. 'Matt may have already gone home,' he said, not really believing his own words. 'We can't risk staying here any longer.'

Sandie dropped to her knees on the sand, tears streaming down her face. 'He's only a boy . . . This is all my fault . . . all of it.'

The peryton's trail was still visible, but it had vanished, directly above Era Mina.

Simon kneeled next to Sandie. 'The peryton will watch out for him. Jeannie says that it's bound to the islands and forever tied to the descendants of the person who first released it. Turns out Jeannie is descended from the first person to animate the peryton. The island is a kind of organic canvas to those descendants.'

'How will that help Matt if he's lost here?' Sandie got to her feet.

'I don't know,' said Simon, 'but we're not helping Em by staying here any longer. Matt is a resourceful kid. He'll be fine. I'm sure of it.'

There was a sudden change in the wind. The mist surrounding Era Mina thickened, then went from pink to green to blue and finally to poppy red. A high white beam of light burst up from the centre of the smaller island like a great, dazzling spotlight.

Clouds of mist stretched into long, thin slivers of colour and wrapped around the beam of light like fingers moulding clay, until suddenly the great light flew towards them in a long, white line stretching from Era Mina to Auchinmurn. Vibrating like a violin string above the water, it created a force of energy that in seconds was churning up a treacherous tidal wave.

As they watched in astonishment, the tsunami suddenly changed its shape, forming a row of silver swords on its crest. The spray was already drenching them. The line of light rose higher, pulling the tide up with it, the blades of the swords stabbing the sky.

'We need to get out of here,' said Simon. 'Now!'

'Not without Matt and Jeannie,' said Sandie. She thrust Em into Simon's arms and began running across the sand.

Simon threw Em over his shoulder in a fireman's hold, chasing Sandie down the beach.

'Jeannie made two copies of the woodcut that brought us here,' he yelled over the roar of the churning sea. 'I've got one and she has the other. Matt came here by some other means. They'll both be able to come home on their own. We have to leave.'

The great wave looked as if it were standing to attention beneath the brightly fluctuating ribbon of light.

'We're not going to survive when this wall comes crashing down,' Simon warned.

'Matt! Jeannie!' Sandie wept. 'I can draw something . . .'

'Don't you get it, Sandie? Jeannie's trying to

protect the island. She's trying to flood it, wash away the sacred relics, destroy the bone quill and *The Book of Beasts* and . . .'

Simon wasn't prepared to share the news of Malcolm's unbinding with Sandie just yet. She was shocked enough about Matt.

'Jeannie's doing everything that she can to secure our futures,' Simon concluded, his voice heavy with emotion. He shifted Em to a more comfortable place on his shoulder. 'If these relics are destroyed, Hollow Earth can't be opened. Ever. Matt will have to look after himself for a while.'

The roar of the wave was becoming deafening. The sea now stood as high as the monastery's towers.

'But what if Jeannie's wrong, Simon? What if nothing changes?' Sandie implored. 'Or worse, *everything* does?'

Simon unfurled Jeannie's second copy of the ancient woodcut of the monastery and reached for Sandie's hand. 'It's a risk we have to take. By tearing up your picture, you and Em will have to return home via 1848, but you told us there's a picture you can use in Duncan's studio to get back to the present, right?'

Sandie slowly pulled her picture from her dress and stared at it. *But what if Matt and Jeannie don't survive the flood?*

The water furled over and into itself until the colossal wave looked like a giant glass locomotive roaring out of the sea towards them.

'I have to find my son!'

Simon thrust Em into Sandie's arms, grabbed Sandie's drawing of the monastery tapestry and tore it up alongside the woodcut Jeannie had made for him. The deluge rushed over the spot where they had stood, slamming into the island a second after they had gone.

High up on the hillside, Jeannie pulled her hands from the cold earth, sat back on her heels and watched her death approaching.

SEVENTY-ONE

The Abbey
Present Day

Em slept fitfully on and off for three long days. When she learned what Matt had done and how Jeannie had followed him to repair the damage, she was inconsolable. She wouldn't eat, she wouldn't read, she stayed in her bed. Her brother was gone, and Jeannie may have drowned. Even Zach was unable to relieve Em's sadness or draw a single smile from her, and it wasn't for lack of trying.

The mood in the Abbey was as sombre as the weather, which had been overcast since their return to the twenty-first century. Simon, Renard and Zach spent their days poring over the maps and tunnel plans that Matt had discovered in the library, determined to find a way back. But it seemed impossible. The tapestry had been destroyed, Jeannie had the original woodcut of the Abbey, and Duncan Fox's medieval watercolour was with Matt. Somehow they had to return to the Middle Ages and undo the damage that their time travel had caused. They had to recover the bone quill and find the rest of *The Book of Beasts* before Malcolm and his monks wrought destruction.

Neither Em nor her mother knew the part that Malcolm had played. The others had decided to

251

keep this information to themselves. How much grief could they ask Sandie and Em to endure?

And so they waited, watching the still-life and all the prints they had found on Matt's desk, hoping that at any moment, Matt would appear, crashing to the floor in a burst of bright colours and even more colourful language. But days passed and Matt never came home.

*   *   *

One morning, later in the week, Sandie marched into her daughter's bedroom, carrying a plate of warm currant scones. Em lay huddled on her bed in the semi-darkness, no handsome knights or pale vampires projecting from her dreams.

'Em,' Sandie said softly, perching on Em's bed. 'Your brother is both resourceful and knowledgeable, and he has Jeannie there with him. They *will* find a way to return. Okay?'

Em sat up against her pillows. 'But what if something happens before then? What if Hollow Earth is opened and—'

'It won't be.'

Sandie set the scones on the bedside table, slipped off her shoes and climbed on the bed with her daughter, pulling Em's duvet over her shoulders. They lay quietly together. In her mother's arms, Em sensed hope and she felt better.

'If anyone can get out of this, Matt can,' Em finally said, allowing herself to feel optimistic for the first time in days. 'If he was stuck forever, lost or dead . . . I would feel it. You know?'

'Of course you would,' said Sandie, climbing from the bed. At the window, she pulled back the

252

curtains. Light flooded into the bedroom.

'I think he'll be fine,' Em said, pushing back the duvet and examining the plate of scones. 'No—I *know* he'll be fine. *You* came back to me, and so will he.'

She picked up a scone and bit into its warm crumbling centre. 'Who made these?' she said as she went to join her mother at the window. 'They're delicious.'

I did.

Em turned. Zach was standing by the door.

I've been watching Jeannie in the kitchen my whole life. Figured I'd have a go.

With a smile, Sandie kissed her daughter, grabbed a scone and left the room.

Zach joined Em at the window, slipping his hand into hers. Together they looked out over the lawns to the bay, and beyond that to the small island, where the sun spilled from a break in the clouds, cloaking the tower of Era Mina in shimmering gold.

GLOSSARY

The Abbey

The Abbey on Auchinmurn Isle started its life as a fortress, then a monastery housing a community of monks in the early Middle Ages, developing into a modern home and place of learning in the twenty-first century. Through time, wars and strife, the buildings and their continuous line of owners have held the islands of Auchinmurn and Era Mina together and kept their secrets safe.

Animare

A person who can animate—bring pictures to life by drawing. The fact of their existence is known only to a few, but there are those who wish to use the powers of Animare for their own evil gain. For this reason, Animare live by the Five Rules:

1. They mustn't animate in public.
2. They must always be in control of their imaginations.
3. If they endanger the secret of their existence, they can be 'bound' (see below).
4. They are forbidden from having children with Guardians (see below), as this can result in dangerous hybrids with an unpredictable mix of powers.
5. Children cannot be bound.

Guardian

A Guardian helps to keep an Animare's powers and emotions under control. Each Animare is allocated a specific Guardian at the age of sixteen. A Guardian's ability to influence an Animare's way of thinking is known as 'inspiriting'. Guardians can use this power on other people as well.

Council of Guardians

A body of Guardians who enforce the Five Rules for Animare. Council members do not always agree about how Animare should be guided. When hybrid children are created, for example, some Guardians believe that their talents should be nurtured, while others believe that binding (see below) is the only safe course of action.

Binding

Binding is a kind of suspended animation. Animare are bound into a work of art as a last resort when they lose control of their powers or endanger the secret of their existence. Binding an Animare can only be authorized by the Council of Guardians, and can only take place when both a Guardian and a second Animare are present.

There are five secure vaults all over the world containing bound paintings. One lies at the Abbey on Auchinmurn Isle.

Hollow Earth

The supernatural place where all monsters, demons, devils and creatures from the dangerous, magical past have been trapped by the medieval monks of the Order of Era Mina (see below).

The Hollow Earth Society

Founded by Duncan Fox in 1848, the original Hollow Earth Society was designed to prevent the world from knowing about the monsters and imagined creatures locked away in Hollow Earth. The reformed Hollow Earth Society has a very different outlook: to retrieve the monsters, control them and unleash them on the world.

The Order of Era Mina

The monks in medieval Auchinmurn belonged to the Order of Era Mina, which had a particular mission: locking away the monsters of the superstitious past by drawing them into a bestiary called *The Book of Beasts*, thereby reinventing the world as a modern place of enlightenment and learning.

ACKNOWLEDGMENTS

Our favourite story as kids was one that our dad would tell us usually on holiday and usually as rain and wind pummelled our caravan. The characters never stayed the same, but the story always ended with a scary chase through the woods and the line, 'Give me back my bone.' In a roundabout way, this book was imagined from that line. So first we need to thank our dad and mum, John and Marion, for always finding time for stories.

To the significant men in our lives, Kevin and Scott, whose unconditional love and unswerving support make our work together possible. We couldn't do this writing stuff without you. To Turner and Clare (Casey too), we miss having you around all the time but love that you're creating your own stories now.

To Lucy Courtenay our amazing editor, whose sharp eye and keen insights helped hone a complicated plot and made this a better book—a huge round of applause.

To the crew at Michael O'Mara Books a big thank you, especially Lesley O'Mara, Alison Parker, Philippa Wingate, Justine Smith, Bryony Jones, Ana McLaughlin and Jessica Barratt.

Special thanks to Gavin Barker of Gavin Barker Associates, Georgina Capel and Anita Land of Capel and Land Ltd and Team Barrowman's Rhys Livesy, Teresa Marsh, Carole Gordon and Gillian

Nuttall.

We're thrilled that the island of Cumbrae has embraced this series and welcomed the Calder twins as their own, but we still have to say that Auchinmurn and its inhabitants (past and present) are creations of our imaginations. Any changes in geography are deliberate and any errors are ours alone.

Finally, we are truly grateful for public art galleries like London's National Gallery, Tate Britain and the Milwaukee Art Museum who have inspired the art in these pages. And we are especially thankful for all who continue to create art and for those who teach us to appreciate it.

Carole & John
2012